The Admiral looked at the sensors, then turned and stared at the calm figure of Dunn. "I don't think you or those who sent you quite realize the situation. You see, we have a Fleet of seven battleships stationed around your planet. All I have to do is give the word, and Kensho will become a smoldering cinder. All life will cease. This is not an idle threat. I will be happy to demonstrate on one of Kensho's moons if anyone doubts our power."

"And yet, Admiral," Dunn replied gently, "I was able to enter this flagship, this bridge, without anyone seeing or stopping me. Think of what that might mean, Admiral . . ."

DENNIS SCHMIDT

WANDERER

ACE SCIENCE FICTION BOOKS
NEW YORK

WANDERER

An Ace Science Fiction Book/published by arrangement with
the author

PRINTING HISTORY
Ace Science Fiction edition/November 1985

ISBN: 0-441-87160-7

Ace Science Fiction Books are published by
The Berkley Publishing Group,
200 Madison Avenue, New York, New York 10016.
PRINTED IN THE UNITED STATES OF AMERICA

This book is dedicated to
my children

☯ Prologue ☯

The mountains rose on every side, dark and lonely in the night. A steady wind blew from the west, shredding the few clouds that clung to the sky and flinging them eastward. Aside from the numbing light of the stars, the night sky was empty.

They sat in a circle, in the center of a plain, in the middle of the mountains. They were nine in number, clad in black, their long gray hair whipping in the wind. Full robes draped and obscured their figures, and deep cowls hid their faces from sight. They sat cross-legged, the skirts of their robes fanning out to cover the ground. There was nothing to indicate who or what manner of creature they might be.

For many minutes, the only thing that could be heard was the moaning of the wind as it swept across the plain and swirled around their circle. Then, as though born of the wind itself, a slightly different sound began to separate itself from the background. It started as the merest whisper. Gradually it grew in intensity, one moment sinking back into the wind, the next rising triumphantly above it. As it rose higher and higher, a light grew on the horizon to the east. Slowly, a moon pushed up between two peaks. Almost immediately it was followed by two more in quick succession. After a short pause, a fourth joined the other three and together they began their march across the sky.

Now the sound was louder and more intense than the wind. Its cadence was wild and irregular, yet seemed to hint at an internal logic that transcended any ordinary concept of order. When softer, it had seemed to come from the very ground itself. Now, as it grew in strength, it could clearly be traced to the circle of figures.

The light of all four moons was surprisingly bright, and revealed something new about the figures. Deep within the cowls were human faces. They were of various forms, but all had the same severe frown of concentration, and the same hard, bright eyes that stared out at things that were not visible. The lips moved slightly, forming the words of the chant that rose to intertwine with the moaning of the wind and swirl off toward the moons slowly climbing in the eastern sky.

The words of the chant were almost recognizable, yet somehow they resisted understanding, twisting from the mind's grasp at the last moment. Higher and higher rose the droning sound until it dominated the night, pulling the wind with it, forcing the clouds to flee, pushing the moons up, up, ever up. The plain, the mountains, and eventually the world began to move around their circle as though around an axis. They were the center.

As the first of the four moons reached the highest point in the heavens, the wordless, flowing chant stopped suddenly and the world was silent in surprise and anticipation. One of the dark figures spoke in a husky whisper that rang out against the mountain peaks. "See! See! It lies there in space, so serene, so beautiful. What shall we call it? What shall its name be?"

"Death," another answered in a dry, rasping voice.

"Life," suggested a second.

"Beginning," came a third answer.

"End," was the fourth.

"Kensho," said a fifth, firmly, commandingly.

Nine heads nodded in agreement. "Yes, Yes. Kensho. For it shall be Death and Life. It shall be Beginning and End. It shall be Kensho. And it shall be Satori."

From the depths of one of the hoods came a cry of pain and horror. "Ahhhhhh! Madness! See how they kill each other!"

"Yesss," came the group's reply. "The Mushin strike, the mind killers, the leeches, the eaters of emotions."

"I am annoyed," one said, a whining complaint in the night.

"Mushin make annoyance into anger," came the muttered answer.

"I am angry," another continued, his voice hard and brittle.

"Mushin make anger into fury," the response hissed.

"I am furious," shouted a third, the very air quivering.

"Mushin make fury into rage."

"I rage, I rage!" shrieked a fourth, his cry splitting the night and causing tiny creatures to huddle in terror in their burrows.

"Now Mushin strike," the chant calmly continued. "Now the killers push the tottering mind over the brink to fall in endless insanity. And now they feed!"

A hideous silence followed, one heavy with dread and death. It was finally broken by a lonely wail. "Dead! Dead, all dead! Bodies everywhere! Twisted, bloody, eyes gouged out, throats torn out. Dead."

"Some live. A few. Those who control the emotions. Those who can still the mind. Nakamura knows. He will save them."

Now a chant rose, soft at first, slowly gaining force until it filled the world with its power. "Moons, moons, shining down on waters, waters moving slowly, moons moving slowly, yet being still. Still the waters, still the moons. Movement, strife, all longing is but a reflection, passing to stillness when the mind is calmed."

The chant ran out into the night, rolling along, smoothing the world. A calm settled over and around the circle. The nine figures were still.

As the second moon reached the height of the sky one of them spoke. "A man comes. And then another. They bring a way."

"Not a weapon, but a Way," the others answered.

"Jerome, to save us from the Mushin."

"Edwyr, to save us from ourselves."

"Way-Farer. He who treads the Way that all may walk it."

"There is Judgment. Those who change survive. The race changes. The race survives."

"Kensho is true to its name. Mushin become Mind Brothers. The ends almost meet, the circle is almost full."

Now the third moon rose to its apex in the night sky. In one mighty cry the circle shouted, "They come! They come!"

The chant ran around the circle again. "With might beyond compare, they come."

"With space-spanning ships, they come."

"With mind twisting machines, they come."

"One comes to Kensho, one goes from Kensho."

"The balance is kept."

"The one who comes, stays, unwhole."

"The one who goes, returns, whole."

"The balance is kept."

"They go." The final words were whispered in tense unison.

For the fourth time, a watchful silence fell over the circle of forms. Though none looked up into the sky, all were watching and waiting for the fourth moon to reach the point already reached by the three others. When it climbed to that place, a great sigh went up from the nine. The sigh changed into a moan that the wind took up and whipped against the mountains until the very air vibrated with it and the ground of the plain trembled and shook.

"Again they come. Many more."

"Yes, yes, they come again."

"Who will stay and who will go?"

"Who will keep the balance?"

"Who will close the circle?"

Eight hooded heads turned to the form at the eastern point of the circle. The cowl dipped slightly and a voice issued forth from its depths. "The past is easily traveled. One road leads back from here. The rest have withered through lack of use. What was is determined by what is. What is contains what must be. This way of seeing can tell no more."

The heads turned then to the figure at the western point. The cowl bowed in acknowledgment and sorrow. "The future is not as open and clear as the past. It is infinite and multitudinous. From this instant the paths of possibility flare off in all directions.

"Once we looked and paid a heavy price. We saw many ends. And some beginnings. Now that which is most probable will be shared. And that which is hoped for as well. Open and receive, for the fourth moon is high and soon will be setting."

The circle breathed deep and drew gently into a stillness that seemed to stop the very flow of time and being. Nothing moved. The wind halted and hung suspended in the frozen moonslight.

Then it was over. The stars went once more on their way, the fourth moon began to set, the wind scurried on eastward in its journey as if to make up for lost time. One of the figures sighed and murmured, "I have seen an end."

"Yes," came the reply, "an end."

"And yet, it was a beginning."

"Yes, a beginning."

"That which has been is always becoming that which will be."

"Through the narrow instant of now the infinite future becomes the singular past. All ends are beginnings, all beginnings ends."

"The moons are setting as soon as they rise."

"The fate of Kensho has risen."

"Now it is setting."

"To rise again?"

"To close the circle?"

A pause followed, one filled almost to bursting with conjecture and wondering. Then with one voice, the nine cried out, "They come, they come, they come!"

Hours later, when the last of the four moons had set, the plain was empty except for the hiss and swirl of the wind. The mountains looked down on darkness. Nothing looked back.

❂ Chapter 1 ❂

The two men seated across the table from each other were a study in contrasts. One was dark of skin, hair, and eye. The other was fair, blond, with eyes of a blue so pale they almost appeared white. The dark one wore a midnight-hued robe, its folds hiding his shape in shadow. His garb was a sign of the high office he held within the Power. It bore no badge or insignia, yet all knew it declared him a Cardinal and one of the Adepts in the faith.

The pale man was dressed in the uniform of a Fleet Admiral of the Home Guard, a simple affair of light blue cut to conform to the figure. The color was in honor of Earth, the incredible water planet that even now looked blue and lovely as it hung in space.

Admiral Knecht watched the man in black with neutral but careful eyes. Cardinal Unduri, he thought, was just possibly the most intelligent, most devious, most dangerous man ever to serve the Power. Everyone knew his story, and he himself relished reminding them of it. Unlike most of those in the Hierarchy, Unduri had not been born into the upper classes on Earth. Instead, he had come from the lowest of slums, the vast, sprawling shantytown that lined both sides of the turgid, foul Congo River. Abandoned by his own parents at an early age, he had fought his way out of the slums and into a minor post in a local chapel of the Power. From that moment on, his rise had been swift, brutal, and nothing short of incredible. His appointment as representative of the Power on this mission was a clear indication of the importance attached to it by the Hierarchy.

As my appointment as military head shows how important *we* think it is, he reminded himself. The whole thing was incredible. He had viewed the tapes himself, many times, and still they made no sense. He had even gained illicit access to the full report of the mind probe the Hierarchy had conducted of Bishop Thwait. The *full* report, not merely the "official" summary the Power had submitted to the Investigating Commission. He shuddered inwardly. They had put one of their own on their damn machines and torn his mind into tiny pieces, searching, searching for the key to what had taken place aboard that scout ship. The results were astounding mainly because they literally made no sense. The whole thing was inexplicable.

No sense, no sense. The phrase echoed in his mind. The ship's tapes made no sense. The memories in Thwait's mind made no sense.

And yet it had happened. The condition of the scout, the crew, and the Bishop all gave grim evidence to that fact. The interior of the ship was blasted and half destroyed. It had barely managed to limp home on its auxiliary systems. But, astonishingly enough, *there was no indication of any external damage!* Whatever had taken place had not been the result of an attack from the outside followed by a boarding.

Which brought up the condition of the crew. More than half had been killed or wounded during the fratricidal conflict that had raged between Admiral Thomas Yamada's men and those who served the Power. Or so it seemed. But such a thing had never happened in the history of the Power or of the Fleet. What in the name of Kuvaz could have caused such a thing? It just didn't make sense. Falling on each other in the face of the enemy? Not one of those questioned could give a satisfactory answer as to what had happened or why they had acted as they did. Several had died under the interrogation, so there was no question of their having held back information.

And then there was the condition of the Bishop himself. The drooling, moaning, crying, terrified shell of Andrew Thwait. What could have plunged a man as tough as

Thwait into raving insanity? What kind of enemy had that scout ship faced?

Which brought him to the strangest part of all. From what he'd seen on the ship's tapes, the enemy was totally unarmed; the planet was inhabited by a culture which was at best a Class Three.

A planet with no weapons, and a girl. The girl Thwait and Yamada had kidnapped to help with the preparation of the spy and for the purpose of "questioning" under the Bishop's machines.

The "spy" had been one Dunn Jameson, an Acolyte Third, Drive Engineer, who had been wiped for heresy against the Power. There had been no details as to the nature of his heresy or about the man himself. These had been erased from the computer's memory when the man's mind had been wiped. After being put on the Power's machines, a person simply ceased existing for all intents and purposes. The Power generally reprogrammed the wiped individual to serve some limited and expendable purpose. In this case he had been turned into a spy. The girl's memories had been used to help program the spy, to give him background on the planet. His mission had been simple: Gather information on the state of military preparedness, and find and kill a person known as the Way-Farer, who was apparently the planet's leader. As interesting as the situation was, Knecht could see no way in which it could have caused the mission's failure. From what the files indicated, the spy had done his job and then had been detonated as usual. No, he thought, Dunn Jameson was an irrelevant factor.

But the girl, the one lone girl. He had watched the tapes of her, the few they had, several times. He had viewed her as she was brought aboard the scout, unconscious and totally vulnerable. He had seen her under the machines. Watched while she had killed four men with her bare hands. Gazed in amazement as she ran through the battling ship, laser rifle spitting death everywhere she went, until finally she reached the communications room and blasted it into molten metal. And then, as an incredible finale, he had seen her disappear into thin air!

What in the name of Kuvaz were they getting themselves into? He looked across the table at the Cardinal. Would he be as much an enemy as the planet toward which they were heading? Would the same thing that had happened to Thwait and Yamada, whatever that was, happen between him and Unduri?

The Admiral cleared his throat slightly and spoke, his voice unusually soft and gentle for a military man. "I, uh, suppose you've familiarized yourself with all the data on the previous mission, your Worship?"

The dark man nodded. "Of course, Admiral, of course." For a few moments, the Cardinal let his gaze rest on the face of the man on the other side of the table. Then he smiled slightly, his eyes glittering coldly in the bluish light that bathed the small room. "I rather imagine we are thinking quite similar thoughts, Admiral. Yes, quite similar." His voice was deep and smooth, soft and totally devoid of emotion. "Thoughts about Thwait and Yamada, about what happened to them above this planet that the girl called Kensho.

"I wonder, Admiral, do you know what that name means, that Kensho? I found it curious that it was nowhere in the report. Apparently, no one found it interesting enough to ask. And that in itself is interesting, no?

"Well, Admiral, my own curiosity compelled me to find out whether it does, indeed, mean anything. And not surprisingly, it does. Most of these Pilgrimage planets are named after the leader of the mission, or perhaps after the group that composed the mission. Quarnon, for example, was so named after the Admiral of the flagship that escorted the Pilgrimage and helped get it established. He died in the process, the victim of a particularly nasty life form the colonists found themselves confronted with. Asaheim, on the other hand, was named after the rather bizarre group that founded it, a group which claimed direct descent from the ancient Norse gods. Strange conceit for a group of mixed northern African stock, wouldn't you say?

"But Kensho? What, in the world, kind of name is that? A true mystery, until I remembered that Nakamura, their leader, was of Japanese descent and a High Master of the

Universal Way of Zen, a minor sect of some fifteen million or so people that regrettably had to be wiped out during the Readjustment.

"Japanese, then, was the clue. Kensho, it seems, was one of the stages of what these primitives called Enlightenment or Satori. It appears—"

"Let's stop the sparring, Unduri," the Admiral interrupted, his voice flat and hard. "Yes, we're both thinking the same thoughts. One of the most disturbing is that I don't think I can trust you and you feel the same about me."

"Ah, Admiral, I admire the directness of your approach. Yes, indeed I do. So military, so forceful. And what you say is true, so true. For, you see, I am aware that you are a member of, as you people put it, the Committee."

The pale man tried hard not to show his surprise. So the bastard knows! But that means the Hierarchy knows! He checked his mind before it went any further in such speculation. There would be time for that later. Right now he had to deal with the man across the table from him.

Before he could reply, however, Unduri lifted his hand to halt him. "Please, Admiral, do not utter a word, either of denial or admission. It is unnecessary, really, and matters not a bit under current circumstances. Let it just stand as concrete evidence of the fact that I fully realize there can be no real trust between the two of us.

"Be that as it may, we find ourselves here together on this flagship, leading a fleet of some seven ships, all destined to envelope and conquer or destroy one tiny planet with a primitive Class Three culture of unknown, but presumably quite dangerous, character. I am here, quite simply, because I am the very best the Power has to offer. And I am sure you are here for similar reasons. Together, we must face this enemy and defeat them.

"I say together because neither of us can do it alone. Now I am quite sure you are intelligent and subtle enough to know precisely what I mean by that, Admiral. And that you are capable of understanding how completely to our mutual benefit it is to cooperate. Not trust each other, by Kuvaz, not for a second. But to cooperate despite our mutual suspicion. To do anything less, I fear, would make us vulnerable to the very fate which befell poor Thomas and Andrew. A fate I, for one, do not wish in the slightest to share."

Unduri watched as the Admiral sat back, stroking his chin in a contemplative motion so typical of the man. *I know you, Knecht, know you almost as well as you know yourself.* Years ago, when the Council of Adepts had discovered the existence of the Committee, each member of the Council had studied two members of the Committee in great depth, trying to learn all they could in the event it became necessary to control or destroy this infantile plot to seize power from the Hierarchy and transfer it to the military. Unduri had drawn Knecht and one other who had died at Quarnon. He had been as relentless in his study as he had been in everything he had ever undertaken for the Power.

The odd thing about Knecht, though, was how little there had been to learn. His past had been totally typical, bland, and rather uninterestingly normal. Unduri had probed and prodded, trying to find strengths, weaknesses, secret sins, anything at all that would give him a handle on the man, a way to intimidate or corrupt him. Most frustratingly, there had been nothing. He had no skeletons in any closets; in fact, he seemed to have no closets! He had no vices and few virtues. Yet somehow he had risen quite high within the military, was considered a brilliant tactician, a competent officer, and one of the most dangerous members of the Committee.

What he's doing right now is a perfect example of how the man operates, the Cardinal mused. *He's sitting there as if considering what I have said. Yet I would swear there isn't a thought going through his mind. Somehow, he decided instantly on my offer and now he's just pretending to consider it because he knows it will look better if he does. I wonder if there really is a man behind those eyes? Could it be nothing but an animate machine?*

The Admiral cleared his throat, dropped his hand back to the top of the table, and said gently, "Yes, Cardinal, I agree. It would be best if we cooperate completely. I am even prepared to trust you. I will tell you what you already

know, but in greater detail. I am a member of the
Committee. That is one of the reasons I was chosen for
this mission. But the strict orders of the Committee are to
forget about the potential conflict between us and the
Power and to concentrate on the more immediate danger,
that is, upon this strange planet and its quite evidently
dangerous inhabitants.

"And now I will show my trust further by telling you the
orders I have received from the High Command regarding
how they wish me to conduct this mission." He paused for
a moment as if trying to remember the exact wording of
the orders. Unduri sat, leaning slightly forward in anticipation, surprised by what the Admiral was doing and not
quite sure why he was doing it. "Mind you, Cardinal,
these orders are not the written ones we both have copies
of. These are the personal ones given to me directly and
orally by the High Commander herself.

"'Knecht,' she said, 'I'm giving you seven battleships.
We had five at Quarnon. The bastards destroyed two of
them. The three left wiped the entire planet from the face
of the universe. You'll have seven. Seven. That's how
important I consider this mission. Now, Knecht,' she
continued, 'you could go in there shooting. Or you could
lay off and play it like Yamada did. I don't like either
option. So here's what I want you to do. Go in shooting,
but only at that old flagship they have. Blast one of the
moons, maybe two. Knock out the biggest population
center you can find. Let 'em know you mean business.
Land a couple of battalions of Marines and have them kill
everything in sight for about fifty miles around their
landing points. Then demand the unconditional surrender
of the planet. If at any time you meet anything resembling
significant resistance, destroy the whole place. Make
Quarnon look like a charity ball. Do you understand?' I
said, 'Yes, sir.' and left."

"The written orders read rather differently, Admiral."

"They do indeed, Cardinal, they do indeed. They
outline standard contact policy. But I tell you this to show
you that I do intend not only to work with you, but to trust
you and share all the knowledge I possess.

"You see, Cardinal, I am fully convinced that this

Kensho represents a deadly threat to our mutual empire. I am further convinced that the planet and every human on it must be either totally subjugated and enslaved or utterly destroyed. There can be no contact, no diplomatic interchange, no mutual trade for mutual benefit, or any of the rest of the verbiage in the standard contact procedures. There can only be total victory for us and total defeat for them. They must be smashed.

"I share this with you openly now, Cardinal, because when the moment comes to act, there will no longer be time to maneuver and negotiate between us. We must strike swiftly and hard, leaving them no opportunity to react. I will not sit out behind some moon as Yamada did and give them any opportunity to do to me what they did to him." Knecht stopped speaking for a moment and gazed at Unduri with his cold stare. "Do you agree, Cardinal? With no reservations, tricks, evasions, second thoughts, or anything at all, do you agree?"

Unduri settled back into his chair, a slight smile turning up the corners of his mouth. "I think we have more to fear from the Committee than we thought. And I also understand completely now why the High Command picked you for this mission.

"Yes, yes, I understand a great deal now. A great deal that needed understanding. Admiral, I thank you for your openness. And I will be as open and as direct myself. My secret orders are quite similar to your own. Kensho must be subjugated or destroyed. And as far as the Power is concerned, destroyed is better. It's so much neater, you know.

"Yes, Admiral, I agree. We shall destroy Kensho. One way or another, we shall destroy it. But now I think we must plan exactly how we intend to go about this task."

For the next two hours, the two men sat in the cold blue light and plotted the death of a world.

⊘ Chapter 2 ⊘

Cardinal Unduri turned off the machine and leaned back into his chair, settling into its comfortable depths and gently rubbing his forehead and temples. He had been going over the files on the Kensho affair once more. How many times did that make? he idly wondered. Two hundred?

Possibly. Perhaps more.

The result, though, was the same as always. Confusion, frustration, and a vague, gnawing fear that he was missing something of critical importance. Something that could mean the difference between the success of this mission and a failure that would be even more spectacular than that of Bishop Thwait.

Cardinal Unduri had known Thwait. Known him well. A competent man, if a bit fanatical and overly impressed with the importance and power of his position. He was bright, but vicious, and sly, so obviously so that it was impossible for him to catch an enemy off guard. All one had to do was look at him to know how dangerous he was.

Yet someone, or something, had been vastly more dangerous than Andrew. More dangerous even than Andrew and an entire scout ship. Could it have been that single girl?

Somehow he doubted it. The girl had obviously been clever, resourceful, tough, and uniquely resistant to the operation of the machines. But it wasn't possible for one girl to defeat . . . or was it? Damnit! That was the whole problem. He simply didn't have enough data to go on!

What about that spy, the one Thwait had sent down to

the planet's surface to kill the Way-Farer? Dunn Jameson. He cursed the Bishop silently. Too damned efficient. He'd erased all record of Jameson when he'd wiped the man for his heresy. By the book, of course, but annoying. Unduri would have liked to know more about this heretic. There was something strange and disturbing about the files on the spy's mission on Kensho. Odd, unexplained discrepancies existed. And there was no firm evidence that the attempt to assassinate the Way-Farer had succeeded. Naturally, the implanted bomb had been exploded, so there was nothing left of the spy, was there? Another unknown. There hadn't been time enough to follow up and be sure. The end of the mission had come too swiftly, too brutally, too finally.

He sighed deeply. So many loose ends, so many unanswered questions. There was simply no way to find out precisely what had happened. Perhaps the Kenshites did have some sort of secret weapon. Who knew?

Even then, he admitted, the physical danger from some secret weapon was not what either he or the Council really feared. No. It wasn't even the whole planet full of people they were speeding toward. The physical force one little, primitive planet could exert made little difference to the vast empire of the Power. Nine planets, billions of people, uncountable wealth. No. It wasn't the physical fact of Kensho that was so threatening.

It was Nakamura. The damned Admiral who had led that mission so many years ago. Led it to Kensho before the Power had achieved its ascendancy on Earth and destroyed all those who refused to accept the holy word of Kuvaz.

Nakamura. A High Master of the Universal Way of Zen. Unduri had indicated to Admiral Knecht that he could find little out about the Zenists. But that was hardly the case. Unduri tapped the console in front of him. With a mere touch on certain keys, he could call up page after page of information on the Zenists. They had been one of the most stubborn and dangerous groups of heretics Kuvaz had been faced with. It had taken years to root them all out and destroy them. Until they had been utterly annihilated, the Power had been insecure.

Oh, there had been other heretics, to be sure. Those who believed that science should be free to explore the universe on its own had rebelled again and again. But they had hardly been dangerous. Their message was too esoteric for the masses and they themselves had seldom been numerous or well organized. All the Power had had to do was catch a few ringleaders, put them under the machines, wipe their minds, and mold new creatures as they would.

But the Zenists, ah, they were a different matter. They believed in things that the Power simply could not allow. Their view of reality left no room for the monopolization of power and knowledge by a single authority. They refused to even recognize authority, claiming that each man must achieve his goal on his own. And worst of all, they claimed that that goal, they called it Buddhahood, could be sought only within the individual because it was already there. The Zenists actually believed that each human being was already perfect and that all he or she had to do was to realize that perfection to achieve it!

Unduri shook his head in angry wonder. Such rubbish! Man was inherently evil, imperfect, weak. It took a strong, central, unquestioned authority to keep him civilized. Without authority, men turned into ravening wolves —raping, pillaging, destroying. Look what they had done on Earth! They had not only destroyed each other again and again throughout history, but had very nearly destroyed their entire planet. Only now, more than a thousand years after the holocausts of the twentieth century, was the planet beginning to blossom again. Trees, yes, *trees* were growing once more! At times, the sky was almost blue. And here and there, the waters were actually clear. That was what the Power had accomplished! That was what authority had achieved!

Most human beings were like children. They had to be watched over and protected, not only from the hazards of life, but from the hazards of each other and of themselves. Too much freedom, too much knowledge was dangerous, even deadly. History had proven that again and again, ad nauseam. Authority, absolute, unquestioned authority was the only way to protect mankind from itself. And that was precisely what the Power, so aptly named by the holy

Kuvaz, provided. And had provided for almost a thousand years.

But what did the damnable Zenists think of authority? One of their own stories told it all. He leaned forward and touched the keys of the console, calling it up from the computer's memory. His eyes ran quickly over the lines. There was no real need to read it. He knew it by heart. Two Zen monks were walking down a dusty road. One asked the other what he would do if the Buddha suddenly appeared in front of them. The other replied that he would instantly prostrate himself and worship the Enlightened One, hoping to be taken on as a disciple. They walked on in silence for a few moments. Finally, the second monk asked the first what *he* would do if the Buddha appeared. The first monk replied that he would spit on him and kick him in the ass.

Or take this example. His fingers flew again and a new story replaced the first. Two monks were walking down a road and in the distance saw several older monks walking in the same direction, away from them. Look, the first one cried, there are some Zen masters! The second monk looked for a moment, then replied, no, those are not Zen masters. How can you tell? demanded the first. The second shrugged and called out, "Masters! Masters! Wait for us!" Those ahead of them stopped and turned around. See, the second monk said, I told you they weren't masters.

Unduri slapped the console and the screen went blank. Heresy! Damnable heresy! To spit on and kick the highest authority! To refuse to accept the authority of acknowledged masters! This was the nonsense that gave birth to chaos!

How could they claim such idiocy? Because they believed that men were inherently perfect, that all they had to do was to discover the perfection within them, that knowledge came from within, through the effort of the individual. And what was the role of the Zen master, or of their own holy literature? Simply to point the way, to bring the individual to the place where he could make the discovery for himself. The Zen master struck the pupil with his staff not to beat the truth into him, but to make

him see the truth that was already there. The master, even
the Buddha, had nothing to offer that was not already
there. The individual brought everything to the party.

Where, then, was room for authority? Where was room
for a force to guide and control the evil in men? Where
was room for the Power and the word of holy Kuvaz?

Yet even that was not the real crux of the matter. At
their very core, the Universal Way of Zen and the word of
the holy Kuvaz were utterly antagonistic. The Zenists saw
the universe as basically perfect and man's role as that of
finding that perfection by peeling away the appearance of
imperfection. The holy Kuvaz, on the other hand, had
realized the ultimate truth that the universe was basically
flawed and that all man could hope to do was salvage what
he could from the maw of incipient chaos. It was man's
duty to impose as much perfection as possible on an
imperfect world. At their very base, then, the two philoso-
phies were totally incompatible and mutually contradic-
tory.

But the Zenists had persisted in their mistaken beliefs.
And the Power had shown the superiority of its truth by
destroying them, by pulling them up, root and all, and
casting them on the fire of utter annihilation known as the
Readjustment. The Power had purified the race of mankind, rid it of fools like Nakamura. Now the Zenists lived
only in the files in the computer. They were no longer
even a memory to the masses of Earth or the other planets of the empire the Power had founded. So what did
that have to do with this miserable little planet called
Kensho?

Because Nakamura had escaped! He had left before the
Readjustment! Because there were other Zenists on that
Pilgrimage! Because it was horribly possible, even likely,
that the ultimate heresy of all still survived on that
accursed planet! Such blasphemy could not be allowed to
live on.

Of course, no one knew for sure that the Zenist heresy
still existed on Kensho. But some of the things the girl,
Myali, had said, and the mind control she had displayed,
indicated the possibility was there. The computer had
given odds in the neighborhood of a thirty-five percent

chance. And that was enough for the Council of Adepts. Kensho had to be destroyed. The danger was simply too great that the evil, if there, might spread.

He wondered what could possibly bring men to believe in such nonsense. He had seen the vileness of humanity at first hand in the slums of Africa. At an early age, his own parents had sold him as a slave to feed themselves and their other children. He had killed his master and his whole family. The tiny fortune he had stolen had launched him on his career. That career itself had been further proof of the evil that lurked inside every human being.

What could bring men to believe there was good in the human soul? History proved just the opposite. Violence, horror, depravity had always been the lot of mankind. Life had been nasty, brutish, and short for the vast majority since the very beginning of time. For that reason, and no other was really necessary, men throughout history had joined together in setting up an authority to rule over them, to force them to be good, to force them to enough peace and security that they might live out their lives in some semblance of safety. Even a despotic authority was better than anarchy. Freedom was anathema to the race, and could only lead to extinction. Nothing but authority could assure the future and make the present livable.

Yet the Zenists denied this. Goodness and truth lie within, they claimed. It is every man's duty to find it within himself and in so doing realize his place in the scheme of things. Only thus can mankind find peace and come to terms with the universe.

What would they have men do? Give up security for knowledge? Give up full stomachs for wisdom? Give up a roof and four walls for goodness? How little they understood human nature!

And still, he knew, they were a danger, and a very grave one. For there were, even now, many who would heed their call, many who would leave the comfort of life under the Power and wander in the wilderness in search of some vague truth, some promise of perfection or unity with the universe. The call of the Zenists reached deep into the human soul and touched something there, something he simply didn't understand. For that reason he hated and feared them. And was determined to destroy them. There was no room in the universe for both the Power and the Zenists. Therefore the blasphemers must be removed. For the good of mankind. And the greater glory of the Power.

Raising his hands, he made the symbol of the Power. "In the name of Reality, in the name of the Circle, in the name of the Power, in the name of Humanity," he intoned with ritual solemnity, "so be it and so it shall be."

Admiral Knecht sat and stared into the empty air of his stark stateroom. He had not told the Cardinal everything the High Commander had said to him. After her first statements, the ones he had related to Unduri, she had gone on, her voice softer, lower, and more confidential. "Knecht," she had said, "the Power is very worried about this Kensho. We don't quite understand why. Despite the failure of the scout mission, it is plain that the planet is a fairly primitive one. It seems unlikely that they represent a very large or very real military threat. All this talk of secret weapons is just so much bullshit and subterfuge. That mission failed from the inside, and the Power knows it."

She had paused for a moment, looking off into the distance. "No, what the Power fears is not something physical," she continued. "They have a very real physical threat right here at home. Us. They know it and take the necessary steps to counteract our power. Quite effectively, I might add. So damned effectively we're helpless to act unless they slip and fall very badly.

"Which must be what makes them fear Kensho. Something about that planet and the people on it bothers them. A lot. Find out what, Knecht. In any way possible. But find out."

For months now he had been working on it, but was no nearer understanding. Through surreptitious means, he had tapped into the Cardinal's data banks and had followed every bit of research the man had done. He now knew as much about Nakamura and the Zenists as Unduri did. None of it made any sense. He simply could not see the threat the Council of Adepts saw. Nakamura had been dead for centuries, and the Zenists extinct for nearly as long. What possible danger could there be in a dead man and a bunch of dead ideas?

Suppose, just for the sake of argument, that the Universal Way of Zen had survived, intact, on Kensho after all these centuries. So what? Surely the Power had infinitely more strength than an extinct religion. It could crush the Zenists, even a whole planetful of them, with ease. Put the whole damn lot under the machines and zap! no more Zenists. Just a bunch of nice, docile slaves. Perfect for working the mines on Sardon III.

No, it wasn't just the survival of a tiny, heretical religion that had the Power frightened. It had to be what that religion represented. He had read the texts in the Cardinal's computer. They seemed utter foolishness to him. "This is the sound of two hands clapping. What is the sound of one hand clapping?" "All existences return to the One. Where does the One itself return to?" "The master asked 'Does the dog have the Buddha nature?' The monk replied, 'Mu!'" "After you have discovered your true nature, then you are able to escape from the cycle of life and death. But when you are about to die, how will you escape?" Nonsense. Sheer, utter trash. What could the Power possibly fear in such drivel?

Yet fear it they did. And greatly. Which meant that perhaps he would have to change his original plans somewhat.

The High Commander had given him two orders. First, destroy Kensho. Second, find out why the Power feared Kensho so much. Clearly the second order was meant to guide the first. He had been told to carry it out in any way possible. That meant even contravening the first order. Not totally, of course. But partially. The first order to destroy Kensho did not specify a time limit. Obviously the second order would determine the time frame of the first. Therefore, he could afford to put off the destruction of the planet until he had had an opportunity to discover why the Power was so frightened. Perhaps when the Cardinal was presented with the planet and its people in the flesh, so to speak, he would let something slip that would give Knecht the clue he needed. In any case, it was worth taking the chance. He would not come in blasting away, raining down destruction indiscriminately. He would calmly and carefully follow the occupation plan, giving Kensho a few hours to capitulate before he attacked or landed troops. During that time he would have Unduri on the bridge with him, and would be able to observe the man's every reaction. It wasn't much, but it was the best he could hope for. A single slip was all he needed.

In the meantime, he would watch the man closely, monitor his every use of his data bank, try to find out all he could. Perhaps he would discover the answer before they got to Kensho. It would be best that way. He'd much rather just blast the planet and have done with it. The idea of sitting out there for even a few hours made him uneasy. He remembered the condition of the scout ship.

The Admiral sighed and stood up. Whatever, he decided. Kensho must be destroyed. Hopefully, its destruction would help the Committee destroy the Power.

☯ Chapter 3 ☯

A lone, brown-robed figure knelt in the dust of the empty yard. The head was bent as if weary, the eyes half shut and staring fixedly at a point about three feet in front of the knees. The right hand rested, palm open and down, on the right thigh. The left arm hung loosely, the sleeve of the robe barely brushing the ground. For long minutes the figure knelt there, the harsh sun of midday turning it into a complex play of light and shadow.

Without warning the head snapped up, eyes sharp and focused. The right foot shot out and slapped firmly on the ground, bringing the figure into a half standing position. At the same instant, the right hand flew to the hilt of the sword that was thrust forward on the left side. With a single sweep, the sword hissed out in an overhand arc. As though it had struck something solid in the midst of the empty air, it stopped short. With a slight pull and a twist, the blade swept free to the right, then around to the front, its point homing in unerringly on the opening of the scabbard. With a decisive snap, it slid home.

The figure returned to its kneeling posture with a sigh and a slight shake of the head. Motionless silence settled over the dusty yard once more.

A hooded form appeared in the opening between the buildings that surrounded the yard. It stopped and gazed toward the kneeling figure, its eyes dark and considering. After a few moments, another similarly draped figure joined the first. The two stood silently watching as the kneeling figure once more drew its sword and slashed at

23

the empty air. The action finished, the two exchanged looks, then turned and walked away together.

"What do you think?" Josh asked the SwordMaster.

The older man looked down at the ground. "He's a very good student. He's strong, fast, well-coordinated, determined. Despite his handicap, he's never once complained or given up." He paused ever so slightly.

"But," Josh prompted.

"But he'll never be a swordsman. At least not in our sense of the word. A technician of the sword, yes. His form is excellent. But a true swordsman, no. He lacks all sense of the sword as anything but an object."

"Have you told him yet?"

The SwordMaster shook his head. "No. It's not something you can tell someone. He has to realize it on his own. That's the only way he'll ever be able to accept it and live with it. It's a pity, really. He has a good deal of talent."

"Still, he's just not one of us," Josh replied.

"No, he's not one of us," the SwordMaster agreed. The two men walked a few steps in silence. "Have we really changed that much, then, Josh? Are we really so different from our ancestors back on Earth?"

Josh nodded. "I'm afraid so. At least that's what the biologists among the Keepers say, after having watched and studied him for the last five years." He motioned with his head to indicate the man they had just left behind. "Oh, nothing visible or obvious. The changes are subtle, primarily in the way our minds function. That's how the species has been evolving here on Kensho." He looked up at the sun, which burned slightly blue in the sky. "Our sun has a higher level of radiation than Earth's and we've had environmental challenges that are radically different."

They walked without speaking until they were almost to the gate of the Brotherhood. The SwordMaster heaved a huge sigh, stopped, and turned to face Josh. "They really are coming, then? There's no possibility that what happened to the scout will scare them off, is there?" Josh's silence was answer enough. "No, I guess not. Wishful thinking, I guess. But still, how many years do we have left?"

"Well, Dunn figured about eight maximum, our time. Five have passed since Thwait and the ship left. They should have arrived at Fleet Headquarters about a year and a half ago. I imagine it took them at least six months to figure out exactly what happened." Josh chuckled humorlessly. "I'm afraid that ship was in pretty bad shape when it left. They would have had to conduct a full inquiry into what took place; especially as to how the Admiral was killed, and how Thwait got in such terrible condition. They undoubtedly had a hard time putting it all together, since they're missing a major piece of the puzzle."

"The Mushin," interjected the SwordMaster.

"Exactly," Josh agreed. "They don't know about the Mushin, don't even suspect their existence. In a very real sense, the Mind Brothers are our secret weapon."

"In a very real sense, Josh," the older man said, "they're our only weapon. If the Fleet comes in here with their guns blazing, we don't have a hope."

"Ah, but that's exactly what they won't do," Josh replied. "The military is highly unlikely to come in blind and fighting after what happened to that scout ship. No, I rather imagine they'll show a great deal of caution. Lay off in deep space and give the whole thing a careful once-over."

"Which is exactly what the scout ship did. Admiral Yamada was no fool."

"Fool or not, there was no way for him to know what he was up against. Any more than our ancestors knew when they first landed here. The Mushin can't be detected by any of the instruments the Fleet carries. The Fleet will be coming in just as blind as Yamada and Thwait did," Josh declared.

"Not quite, my Son. They already know something went wrong the first time. If they can't find any indication of what that something could be, they'll be even more alert and ready for surprises. They'll be nervous and ready to shoot at anything." He shook his head sadly. "I'm worried, Josh. Worried that they'll shoot first and ask questions later . . . of the cinders."

Josh frowned. "That's possible, I admit, but—"

"And even if they don't," the older man interrupted,

"even if they sit out there like the scout did, hiding behind one of the moons, just waiting and watching, what can we do against them? We have no weapons to match theirs." He touched the hilt of the sword that was thrust through the sash tied around his waist. "The sword is a wonderful weapon. It trains the body, the mind, the spirit. But against a laser blaster, well . . ." He shook his head again. "The most we can hope for is a noble, if fruitless death."

The younger man looked deeply into the eyes of the older. There was no fear there, only a soft and sad acceptance of fate. This man would literally charge a laser cannon with his sword if he had to. And die without a murmur of complaint. "I don't think it's as hopeless as all that, Master," Josh said quietly. "We may have a great deal more going for us than a few swords."

The SwordMaster shrugged. "We defeated one scout ship. But we had total surprise on our side, and a virtual insurrection aboard the ship. This time we won't have either."

"True," Josh replied. "But last time we didn't know anything about our enemy. And we do have the Mind Brothers."

"You would use the Mushin against the Fleet?" the older man asked.

"It's a possibility," Josh said defensively.

The SwordMaster smiled. "True. A possibility. Except that we have to get the Mushin to the Fleet. Last time we had Myali aboard, Josh. I doubt they'll make that error again.

"And even if we did get the Mind Brothers aboard the ships of the Fleet, my Son, how could we be sure that the result of the ensuing insanity wouldn't merely be an instant and devastating attack against Kensho rather than mutual slaughter?"

Josh looked thoughtful. "Hmmmmmm. We couldn't. Still, I feel the Mushin are an important factor in our favor. Somehow . . . somehow . . ."

"Perhaps, perhaps," nodded the older man. "I'm just glad you're worrying about it and not me. I've enough problems with this new crop of students. Ah, all they talk about is the Fleet coming from Earth and how we'll fight them from tree to tree and door to door all across the face of Kensho. Huh. As if there'll even be a Kensho left to fight over once they're through." With a final wave, the SwordMaster turned and walked off.

For several moments Josh stood and watched him go. His mind poked and prodded at the question that had occupied him for the last five years. How could they meet the might of Earth's fleet when it burst out of Aspect-Sarfatti drive and into Kensho's system? There had to be a way! In one fashion or another, almost everyone on the planet had been working on that problem. Some had been seeking to copy the Earth weapons, especially the laser wand which Dunn had tried to use to assassinate the Way-Farer. Others had been busy searching for new weapons, weapons different from those of Earth.

The progress had been astounding. In a few short years, they had mimicked an incredible amount of Earth's weapon technology. If they had, say, ten more years and unlimited resources, they might be able to equal the force of the Fleet they knew was on its way. Of course, they didn't have that much time. And to develop the resources meant doing things to Kensho that made him shudder with horror.

So much accomplished. So much yet to do. The worst thing about it all was that Josh wasn't even sure they were on the right track. Despite all the progress, he had the nagging feeling they were overlooking something critically important. And he was convinced it had something to do with the Mind Brothers, the Mushin, the mind leeches that had almost destroyed the people of Kensho. Nakamura had managed to use them to save humanity from its first crisis. All he had to do was follow Nakamura's example. He chuckled silently. That's all. Just follow the example of one of the greatest geniuses of all time! Nothing to it!

Thinking about Nakamura reminded him of the koan the man had left behind. Every generation since then had wrestled with its meaning, giving it new and different

interpretations according to the problems they faced.
Could it hold an answer for us, too? he wondered. Let's
see, it goes:

> To be free, a man must follow the Way
> that leads to the place where he dwelt
> before he was born.

He let it roll around in his mind for a few moments. Must
give it more thought, he decided. There's something
there . . . something . . .

Then another koan came to him, equally enigmatic,
equally puzzled over in the history of Kensho—Jerome's
koan:

> As the Ronin strikes,
> oh, how beautiful
> the constant stars.

Was there a hint there, too? A resonance that struck
something deep inside him?

Yes, definitely. But what? And how could he translate it
into something useful, something that would help Kensho
defeat a heavily armed fleet from Earth? His mind went
round and round the problem as it had for the last five
years. There seemed no way out. But, he knew, that was
precisely the purpose of koans. There was no way out of
them. They were supposed to drive you to the edge of
despair, to the point where you gave up all hope of
figuring them out. There was no logic in them. They were
a device used to force the mind beyond the logical, beyond
the sane. They twisted and turned the mind, exhausting it,
beating it down until it was ready to open to new and
greater meaning, meaning that lay beyond logic, sanity,
common sense. That meaning was known as Enlightenment, or Satori.

Yet Satori, he knew, was not problem specific. It did not
provide answers. It simply changed utterly the way one
saw the problem. Perhaps that is what I need, he thought.
Perhaps I'm not seeing the problem from the right angle.
His mind spun with confusing, conflicting thoughts. How
can I get where I want to go? I must do something drastic.
But what?

He walked slowly through the gate of the Brotherhood. In the distance he could see the hills rising blue-green toward the horizon. So beautiful, he thought, so beautiful. Aimlessly, deep in thought, he began to wander generally westward.

Josh, a voice said in his mind. *The Council's meeting. We're going to Snatch you. Ready?* He sent back an affirmative reply and disappeared with a slight pop.

⊗ Chapter 4 ⊗

The sword hissed from its scabbard and sliced the air. Halfway through its arc another blade met it with a ringing clash. Cautiously, the two weapons parted and the men wielding them looked appraisingly at each other over the intervening space.

"Good," the gray-haired one grunted. "Fast and precise. Perfect form. Now we'll see if you have more than form." With a sudden move his sword flicked out toward the other man's throat. Steel rang on steel again as the first man parried and slashed back at the other man's wrists. The gray head nodded in satisfaction. "Huh. Not bad."

The first man took a step back, his sword in mid-onguard position, his blue-green eyes wary. His six-foot, well-muscled body was relaxed, yet ready for instant action. Sweat trickled down his face from under an unruly bush of curly, reddish-blond hair. He said nothing as the gray-haired man slowly moved to the left, looking for an opening.

"I think," the older man said as he stepped, soft and careful as a cat, "that you are doing better today than you ever have in your life. Still, I wonder. I wonder if you really are letting yourself go. We shall see. We shall . . ."

Halfway through the sentence, he struck with an overhand sweep toward the head. As the younger man raised his sword to block, however, he changed his attack, stepping suddenly to the side and aiming a blow at the hand that held the sword. The move caught the other by surprise and he tried to step back out of the way. The older man again changed his assault in midair, ignoring the original target and driving a thrust for the throat. The blade darted out like a striking snake and lightly touched the young man's adam's apple, drawing a slight trickle of blood.

"You're dead, Dunn," the SwordMaster said solemnly.

His face blank with surprise, Dunn sheathed his sword and reached up to touch his throat. He looked at the tiny smear of blood on his fingertips. "Huh," he grunted. "Yeh. I see. Damn! That's the way it always is! No matter what I do you kill me. I'll never get this," he muttered, looking down at the dusty earth of the practice yard in disgust. "I practice for hours and still it comes out the same. I can block two or three of your attacks, but then you do some fancy combination, I can't keep up, and I get killed."

The SwordMaster stood silent, watching him carefully. Dunn looked up and their eyes met. For several moments they stood thus, neither one speaking. Then Dunn nodded. "So," he said, "that's the way it is, I guess. I never will get it, will I? Don't bother with formalities. Just say it."

The old man sighed. "Never is a long time, Dunn. But, no, I don't think you ever will 'get it,' as you say. You see, it's not just a matter of practice, though the Gods only know we all practice enough for it to seem so. It's more . . . well, practice is just a way to learn the technique until we know it so well we can forget it. And go beyond it."

Dunn shook his head. "And that takes something I don't have doesn't it? And I don't mean my missing hand, either," he said, lifting up his left arm so that the sleeve fell back to reveal the stump where his hand had once been. "No, it's not just that. It's something you here on Kensho are born with. Oh, I know, Master, I know." He pointed toward his head. "Don't forget that I've got part of one of you right inside here, telling me what I'm doing wrong. Only problem is, she can't tell me how to do it right. Or at least not in any way that makes sense to me.

"Well," he continued, looking vaguely around the

empty practice yard, "Power knows I've tried. For five years, I've tried." He fixed his gaze on the SwordMaster again. "But I'm not going to make it, am I?" he asked one more time, as if hoping that somehow the answer might change.

The older man looked him firmly in the eye. There was a sadness in his glance, but there was no question as to the finality of what he said. "No, Dunn. You're not going to make it. You'll never be anything but a technician of the sword. Never a swordsman."

"Never one of you," Dunn countered, a slight edge of bitterness entering his voice. "Just an Earthman light-years from home on a planet where he doesn't belong."

"You belong here, my Son," the SwordMaster protested. "We all—"

"You're all honored to have me. I know, I know. But then you really haven't much choice, have you? Admiral Yamada and Bishop Thwait dumped me here to spy on you and kill the Way-Farer. I failed in those two—"

"Dunn," the older man interrupted sternly, "you didn't fail. You succeeded in breaking away from a servitude more total, more brutal than anything any of us have ever experienced. By the Gods, man, they wiped your mind! But you fought back! You cut off your own hand to beat them! Your humanity won out over their brute, inhuman power and you . . . Well, I would hardly call what you accomplished a failure, my Son."

The younger man looked down at the ground. "Oh, yes, with the help of Myali and the other things that crowded in my mind I won that victory." He lifted his eyes and gazed directly into those of the SwordMaster. Slowly he lifted the stump of his left wrist until it was between them. "I won that victory and paid a very dear price for it. And all of you won, too. I bought time for you, made the Bishop and the Admiral think that their plans were going well. But they weren't, were they? Not even from the start.

"You knew I was here. Knew I was here and why from the very beginning. No, don't deny it. Don't bother. It doesn't matter. I've thought about it a lot. You see, I was landed in a clearing, I know that. But I didn't wake up in a clearing. You people moved me. You were there right from the beginning and probably kept a watch on me the whole time."

He barked a short, harsh laugh. "Thwait and Yamada sent me down here for purposes of their own. You people outthought them and used me for purposes of your own, all the time letting them think it was going their way. You bought time so Myali could find out what was going on aboard the scout and find some way to disrupt the mission. The whole time I was struggling to break free of the Spy and my conditioning I was just a pawn in someone else's game!"

"But you did break free, Dunn," the old man said gently. "You defeated them and found your way back to yourself."

Dunn shook his head in doubt. "I don't even know about that. It wasn't just me. Myali was there in my mind, Myali and that other thing. I don't really know who or what gave me the strength to break Thwait's control. In any case, the result was exactly what you all wanted. I . . ." He took a deep breath and let it out slowly. "Ahhhh, look, Master, I'm . . . I'm afraid it's all a bit too much for me right now. I . . . I need to think. Oh, hell, I guess I've known deep inside I wasn't going to make it for some time now. But, well, now that it's out in the open it's not quite as easy to live with as I thought it might be. I . . . I need time to think."

The SwordMaster put his hand on Dunn's shoulder. "I understand, my Son." He dropped his hand, bowed slightly and walked slowly away.

Dunn remained motionless and wordless, staring after the old man until he disappeared between the buildings that surrounded the practice yard. Then he turned and walked at a weary pace in the opposite direction. As he approached the open shed where the practice gear was stored, he halted. He looked down at the sword that was thrust through the sash that circled his waist. After a moment of quiet contemplation, he drew it out, scabbard and all, and held it up to eye level. It was about two inches shorter than a regular sword and slightly lighter, as befitted a weapon to be wielded with one hand. Most of the Kenshites used the longer two-handed sword, though

a few preferred the smaller weapon combined with an
even shorter and lighter one in the other hand. He didn't
have another hand.

Should I leave it here? he wondered. It was made
especially for me, but I've no real right to it. He stepped
forward, about to hang it on the pegs in the shed. At the
last moment, though, he stopped and drew back, staring
at the sword. No, damnit, he thought. I've sweated over
this sword for five years. It's as much a part of me as
anything is. It's mine. I've earned it. I may not be able to
use it as well as the rest of them, but it's legitimately mine
and I'll keep it.

Wherever I go.

For the first time he realized that he intended to go.
Where? he asked himself. Does it really matter? he
replied. He snorted. Huh! Still holding dialogues in my
head. Only at least now there's only one voice and I
control it. Sort of.

I'm going, he told himself again. Not back home, of
course. Earth is a bit far to walk. Not anywhere in
particular, in fact. I'm just going to go. Like the Kenshites
do at times when things get to be too much. Like Myali
did.

Yeh. When things get to be too much. They're too much
all right. And it's high time I went off someplace nice and
far away to think them over for a while. Hell, I've got a
good two or three years to think before the Fleet comes
back. After that, well, by the Power, thinking won't be
much in demand anyway. Neither will anything else, for
that matter.

He tucked the sheathed sword back into his waistband,
squared his shoulders and looked around as if he had just
woken from a long sleep. The yard looked different
somehow, now that he was leaving. I never really looked
at it, he realized. I was always so busy doing something
that I never really saw what was around me. I wonder how
many other things I've failed to see in the last five years?

Well, he said silently to the practice yard, so long. I
never really got to know you. Have to say good-bye to
some other folks, though, so I won't have time now and I

kind of doubt I'll be back. Spent a long time here. Maybe
a little too long. He turned and strode out of the yard.

His first stop was with Father Johnston, the head of the
Brotherhood where he had spent the last five years. He
found the ancient little man seated in full lotus posture in
the middle of the floor of his cell. Johnston had been
meditating, but he looked up as Dunn approached.

"So, leavin', eh?" the tiny man piped in his birdlike
voice. He cocked his head to one side and gave Dunn a
quick smile. "Thought you'd be, one of these days. Yep,
time you was off on your Wanderin'. Need it, Dunn. We
all do, some time or other. Things just seem to pile up and
the only answer is to take to Wanderin'. Damn if I'm not
thinkin' of doin' it myself. Gettin' just a wee bit weary, I
am, of stickin' round this 'hood taking care of all these
Fathers and Brothers and Novices. Damn nuisance, the
whole lot of 'em."

Dunn turned his head to hide his smile. The old man
always complained about his duties as head of the Brotherhood, but Dunn knew he loved them. And every one of
the Fathers and Brothers and Novices as well. Me, too, he
suddenly realized. He loves me, too. That's what all this
banter is about. He's upset because I'm leaving, because I
have to go.

He raised his eyes to meet those of the old man. Behind
the hard, birdlike luster of the sharp stare was a softness
he had never noticed before. He felt suddenly ashamed. I
never really understood.

He started to speak, but the little man held up a thin
hand to forestall him. "Hush, now, lad. I know what
you're thinkin' even before you think it. No need to say a
thing.

"It's been hard on you, it has, Dunn. You're not one of
us and yet in so many ways you're more like us than you
are like your own kind. You've tried, lad. Gods know,
you've tried. I've watched you 'til I've ached."

"I'm not one of you," Dunn repeated slowly and softly.
"I'm not really one of anything."

"That's where you're wrong, lad. Dead wrong. You're
one of yourself, that you are for sure. Only trouble is,

although you've broken free of the controls they put on you, you've still not really found out who you are. So, though you're part of yourself, you don't really know what you're part of.

"Centuries ago, lad, a very wise man on Earth said that the most important thing was to know yourself. His race even wrote that as a motto over the entrance to one of their most sacred temples. 'Course, he couldn't have had your precise dilemma in mind, but your problem is much more common than you might think on first thinkin'.

"One way or other, Dunn, we all have it. Not as that offers much comfort, I know. But the thing you're sufferin' from is something we all agonize over at some time or other. That is, we do if we're worth anything! Aren't any standard answers, either. Just have to live through the pain of findin' your own. Some make it. Some try and fail, but learn to live with the pain of not knowin'. Others just give up. Those are the ones to be sorry for.

"But you, now, lad, you'll not be givin' up, that I'm sure of. Thwait and all his fancy machinery couldn't beat you. You'll either find your answer or learn to live with the pain of not knowin'.

"Hmmmmm," he looked down at the mat he sat on. "Blatherin' like a dotard, that's all I'm doin'. Lad's made up his own mind. Knows what the problem is. And I sit here and blather at him. Whew! Must be gettin' old, losin' my grip." He looked up at the young man who stood towering over him, a slight smile creasing his old face. "'Course there'd be others you'll be wantin' to say goodbye to, so I'll not be keepin' you any longer, lad. Jerome walk with you, my boy. And may your Way be smooth." He nodded and turned away, immediately returning to his meditation.

Others I'll be wanting to say good-bye to, Dunn thought. Oh yes, there are others. Those good-byes would not be as easy to say as the ones to the practice yard and Father Johnston.

❧ Chapter 5 ❧

"I'm worried about him."

Josh glanced up at his sister. The afternoon light slanted across her face, emphasizing the frown that knit her forehead and the lines at the corners of her eyes. She's aged in the last five years, he realized suddenly. Aged more than five years' worth.

He looked into her eyes. More than her face had aged. The things that Bishop Thwait and his machines had done to her on that scout ship had clearly affected her to the very core of her being. What have they done to you, little sister? he wondered.

He remembered the morning five years ago just before she had left on her mission. He had looked into her eyes then, too, and had seen doubt, confusion, and barely repressed fear. Plus a firmness of purpose that had made his plea to her not to go seem a foolish, shallow thing. He hadn't been surprised when it had fallen on deaf ears.

So she had gone, all alone, to the scout ship that lurked behind one of the moons of Kensho. And there Bishop Thwait had battered and twisted her mind with his machines.

Somehow she had survived. No, more than survived. She had triumphed. His little sister had beaten the Admiral, the Bishop, the machines, the whole ship, and sent the lot limping back home.

Whatever had happened, however it had taken place, it had changed Myali. In place of the old confusion and fear, there was a new calmness and firmness. Clearly, she had made the leap into the awful Void and falling, had found her wings.

But there was more. There was a depth, a depth that made him uncomfortable if he stared into it for very long. He shuddered suddenly. *She has gone places none of us on this planet have ever been. And suffered things none of us have ever felt.*

She was not the Myali who had left that morning more than five years ago, the frightened girl who had gone, totally alone, to fight for her whole planet aboard an alien spaceship. And yet, she was the same in so many ways. The slight frown, the serious way of looking at him, the intensity with which she tackled things. It *was* Myali. But Myali broader and deeper than he could reach or even comprehend.

His mind turned back to what she had just said. "Worried?" he murmured. "About Dunn?" She nodded silently and continued looking at him. Josh moved uncomfortably under her stare. "Uh, well, what are you worried about?"

She sighed. "Josh, you know very well what I'm worried about. I'd be willing to bet you've already discussed it with the SwordMaster."

"Hmmmm. You know too much, little sister, for someone who hasn't even been here for a good two months. How are preparations going?"

"They aren't. And don't try to change the subject. What about Dunn?"

"Dunn. Yes." He looked down at the ground, then back up at his sister. "He won't make it, Myali. He'll never be a swordsman. No matter how hard he tries, he's just not one of us."

She stared at him for a moment before answering. "I know he's not one of us in the genetic sense, Josh, but I don't for a moment believe he can't become one of us in the spiritual sense. After all, Nakamura wasn't one of us genetically, either. I hardly think you'd judge him incapable of entering and passing through the Void as easily and adeptly as any of us.

"Certainly our genes make it easier for us, almost inevitable in fact. For generations, we've used the Judgment to weed out those without the proper genes before they even have a chance to grow up and pass along their defects.

"But we shouldn't let that blind us to the fact that ours isn't the only way to achieve Satori. We should never forget that, Josh. Ours isn't the only way."

"Myali," he said softly, gently, "he'll never be a swordsman. Maybe he can find some other path, but he will never be able to walk the Way of the Sword." He shook his head sadly. "Do you have any idea of the mess his mind is in? He managed to break through his conditioning and find himself. At least part of himself. A good portion of the original Dunn was simply destroyed by Thwait and his machines.

"That isn't enough, Myali. You're still inside him. You, and some other things even he doesn't understand.

"Don't you see? Dunn can't become a swordsman, can't reach Satori, because *there is no Dunn*. There's only a collection of things more or less under the control of something that currently calls itself Dunn. Nothing that fragmentary, that confused, can generate the kind of concentration and centeredness it takes to make a swordsman, much less to break through to Satori.

"He's tried, Myali, tried and tried and tried. It's enough to make you weep. I've watched him out in the practice yard drawing and cutting for hours. I've seen him doing his kata over and over, repeating blocks and cuts until my body aches to even think of the effort he's putting forth.

"None of that changes the fact that he never goes beyond a certain point. Oh, he's a good technician. I'd wager he could handle most Ronin. But . . ." he shrugged in conclusion.

A silence fell between them. Josh watched Myali as she stared off into the afternoon sky. Eventually, she spoke in a soft, almost whispery voice. "Has anyone told him?"

"No. The SwordMaster is hoping he'll realize it on his own."

"Will he?"

"I think so."

"What will happen to him then?"

Josh met her eyes. "I don't know." He turned away,

looking back toward the Brotherhood which stood below
them in the valley. It had been there, almost unchanged,
ever since the time of Jerome. Many of the 'hoods had
been destroyed when the Kenshites had broken free of the
Grandfathers and the control of the Mushin, shattered by
the very Brothers and Sisters who had lived within their
walls. They had been driven mad by the Mind Leeches
and, like their ancestors so many years before, had
slaughtered each other indiscriminately. The survivors
had abandoned the Way of Passivity and followed the new
Way that Jerome had brought. Now the Mushin were
under control, so much so that they were referred to as the
Mind Brothers. Mankind had spread across the face of
Kensho.

As he mused, he noticed a figure leaving the gate of the
'hood and coming in their direction. He motioned to
Myali, and she looked too. He cocked a quizzical eyebrow
in her direction and she nodded. It was Dunn. Josh turned
as if to leave, but his sister touched his sleeve bidding him
stay.

Long before he could see Dunn's face, he knew. The
question as to what the Earthman would do once he
realized he would never be a swordsman was about to be
answered. He glanced over at his sister and saw that she
had seen what he had noticed. A look of concern and pity
passed briefly over her face, then melted away to be
replaced by that bottomless calm he had noticed before.

Dunn halted about ten feet from them and stood quietly
for several moments. Josh could sense the agitation just
beneath the silent surface, and knew the man was struggling for control.

"I'm leaving," he said abruptly.

"Where are you going?" Myali asked softly.

He shrugged. "No place in particular. Home is too far
to walk. I'm just going."

"Wandering?" Josh suggested.

"Sure. Why not? That's as good a name for it as
anything else," Dunn replied, a slight edge of bitterness
creeping into his voice. "Look, what do you say we cut
through all this and just say it out straight? I'm leaving
because there's no reason to stay anymore. I'll never be a

swordsman no matter how long I sweat in that practice yard. I know I'm welcome to stay as long as I want. I'm a national hero. The guy who didn't kill the Way-Farer. But I don't belong here at this 'hood, here where everybody is following the Way and getting somewhere. So . . . so I'm leaving." Dunn raised his eyes to meet Myali's. Their gazes touched and locked. Suddenly, they were talking only to each other and no one else existed.

"Five years, Myali. I've tried for five years. This last one has been hell. Just as it all seemed to be coming together, it fell apart again. I . . . I've gotten very confused at times. I've lost my direction so often. It's hard to explain. I've wanted things I can't even define, had yearnings I can't express, experienced fears I don't understand. Nothing seems to fit anymore. Me least of all."

"You never told me, Dunn."

"It's not exactly the kind of thing you can share, Myali."

"But I've sensed it and watched the secret pain grow in your eyes, even when you looked at me."

Dunn's eyes wavered and dropped to gaze at the grass that grew on the hillside. "Yes," he replied, his voice a husky whisper, "even when I look at you. Or especially when I look at you."

His head came back up slowly, and he looked deeply into her eyes. "I love you, Myali," he said softly. "You know that. You're part of me in a way no woman has ever been part of a man before. For a long time, your love was the only thing that kept me going here on Kensho. I was determined to be worthy of you, to make you proud of me, to become a swordsman and one of you.

"But I can't, you see. I know that now. I can't be one of you and no amount of love or pity or anything else can change that. And I fear what will happen to our love, what it will become. I know it can't stay the way it was, know it was changing already. I . . . I . . ."

"Can't I just love Dunn as he is rather than as he would be?" Myali asked.

Dunn's lips twisted in a half smile. He barked a harsh laugh. "As I am? What am I, Myali? What is this Dunn that stands before you? A good part of me is you. Here and there are pieces of the man who grew up in the service of the Power. There are other things, too. Things lurking in the dark spaces and the gaps. Is it any wonder I can't be one of you? I can't even be one with myself!

"No. Don't talk of loving me as I am, Myali. At best, you'd be loving something only half formed. Good-bye, Myali. Thank you." He turned suddenly to Josh and held out his hand. "Good-bye to you, too, Josh." With that, he turned and walked off, away from them and away from the 'hood in the valley. For the first time, Josh noticed that he had a knapsack on his back. Dunn was leaving. He was leaving now.

Josh looked at his sister. Her gaze was level and calm. "Should we . . . ? he began.

She waved him to silence. They stood and watched the figure of Dunn disappear over one hill, then rise up the side of another, then disappear again until finally he was gone. The Earthman was heading south-southwest.

Myali turned back to him. "It's right. He must go. Alone. His bitterness is natural. Until he works through it on his own it will stand in his way. He must find out who and what he is before he can reach the end of his path."

"Can he do it, Myali? I mean, the Mushin and the Ronin and—"

"He has to try. We all run that risk, Josh. Remember the Judgment. As tiny children we must show our ability to survive here on Kensho. If we are deficient, we die. Dunn has the right to prove his own fitness in his own way. And he's had five years of the best training there is. I suspect his control is probably better than either of us think. No, I don't believe he'll become a feast for the first passing Mushin. Nor the victim of the first Ronin he meets."

Josh shook his head doubtfully. "Training in a 'hood is one thing, little sister, and real experience is another. The Mind Brothers in the 'hood are firmly under the control of the Fathers and Brothers. A mistake in the practice yard may be a source of embarrassment, but it's not likely to be fatal. He's out in a very real world now, one that doesn't tolerate even little mistakes. What if he dies?"

"Then he dies knowing that he tried."

"Myali, you're asking him to do what Jerome did! But without Jerome's natural abilities."

She looked at her brother for a few moments before replying. "We all go to the place where we dwelt before we were born, Josh. Some go while alive. Some die to get there. Do you think that those babies who fail in the Judgment achieve it any less than you and I do?"

He turned away and looked off toward the point on the horizon where Dunn had finally disappeared. When he looked at her again his face was still, but there was a gleam of wonder and curiosity in his eyes. "You've changed even more than I thought, little sister. Perhaps more than I can even understand. Can I ask you a question?" She nodded. "Did you ever love him, Myali?"

A slow smile spread over her face. "I'm part of him in a way no woman has ever been part of a man before," she said gently. Then she turned and started off down into the valley where the 'hood lay in the growing shadows of late afternoon.

Josh stood and watched her go. Did she answer me? he wondered.

✿ Chapter 6 ✿

With a sharp hiss and a whoosh, the bush burst into flame and disappeared. No one seemed surprised.

"Ah," said the Way-Farer softly, almost as if breathing the word. "It works."

"Yes, Father, it works. We based the mechanism on the laser wand Dunn used to attempt his assassination of you."

"You mean the one with which he cut off his own hand."

"Yes, Father. That's what I meant. Sorry."

Father Kadir, the Way-Farer, waved his hand to dismiss the entire thing. "No matter. How many of these can we make and what will the cost be to our planet?"

The young man thought for a few moments. "Well, the first question is easily answered. We have about three years, and I estimate we could manufacture, oh, say, several thousand hand lasers and maybe a hundred or so cannons in that time."

"Hmmmm," commented one of the other members of of the Council. "Hardly enough to do battle with a Fleet."

"Hardly," the young man agreed. "And even then, we could only fight once the Fleet has landed. We have absolutely no capacity to mount off-planet defenses, even if we revive the flagship."

A short, round woman from the southern continent spoke up. "And what would the cost be? In terms of tearing up Kensho and filling the skies with foulness?"

The young man looked at Josh and received a nod.

44

"Well," he began, "the price would be pretty heavy. We'd need to mine metal and several other things. And—"

Kadir held up his hand to halt the recital. "There's no need to go into detail. We've all studied your report. I think what Mother Cathe had in mind by her question was more whether you thought the cost worth it."

"Well, I . . . I mean, I'm not really in any position to pass judgment. I mean, I'm only a technician, a kind of Artisan-Keeper. I'm not even one of the Council."

"This is your planet, too, my Son. Any decision made will affect everyone on Kensho. Being members of the Council doesn't give us any edge in wisdom."

The young man shifted uncomfortably. "Well . . . I . . . of course I'd like to fight the Fleet. I mean, we can't just let them walk in here and take over. This project," he held up the laser pistol, "I've spent the last five years of my life working on it, trying to find a way to help us match, even slightly, the power that Earth will bring against us. I . . . I want to fight." He looked at the pistol in his hand, then up at the rolling hills that stretched off in all directions from the hilltop where they sat in council. Here and there, groves of stately trees filled the hollows between the hills, occasionally running up the sides and even covering the crowns. Overhead, the sky arched clear and blue, the color even more intense given the bluish cast of Kensho's sun.

Finally, his eyes came to rest on those of Father Kadir. The Way-Farer's eyes were black, deep, and calm. The hooked nose and the thin lips betrayed no hint of emotion. His black hair, slightly graying at the temples, gave him a reserved and distinguished air. Both his hands, usually mobile and alive when he talked, lay quietly in his lap as he waited to hear the young man's opinion.

"I want to fight," he repeated. "But at what cost?" His voice dropped and became husky. "At what cost, Father? Must we rape our Kensho to make weapons? Must a fourth of our people die in battle? A half? All?

"Yet I can't help but wonder what choice we have. Surely the Fleet won't come back and peacefully negotiate with us, offering us equal place with honor in their empire? They'll come to enslave us, or destroy us utterly.

"What are we to do? Submit without fighting? Arm and tear Kensho apart with our arming, then fight and lose anyway? I . . . I've thought about it for the last five years while I've worked on the project. Oh, I admit that at first I was all for fighting to the last man. That seems so futile now." He looked down at the weapon in his hands. "It all seems so futile."

A slender man from the Plain spoke out, anger edging his voice. "Futile? How can it be futile to fight? Would you have us sit back and let them do as they wish?" He turned to the rest of the Council. "Didn't their last mission show us what kind of people they are? They will annihilate us if we cannot fight back."

"No one's saying we shouldn't fight back, Judah," Josh replied. "We all want to fight back. I just wonder if the best way to fight them is on their own terms."

"What do you mean?" Judah asked.

"Well, this laser pistol, for instance. This is fighting them the way they expect to be fought. It's the way they fight. They're experts at it. At best, we're beginners. What's more, we can't even begin to match their fire-power. The outcome is, you'll pardon me, Judah, inevitable and not in our favor. We might manage to die grandly, but we would die. All of us. And to be honest about it, I doubt we would even die grandly. I rather imagine that at the first sign of resistance, they'll just sit off-planet, where we can't reach them with our limited weapons, and blast us with missiles and whatnot until there isn't a thing left alive on the face of Kensho. Not only will we die, but so will our planet.

"No, I really don't think we can afford to fight them on their own terms. We have to think like Nakamura did when faced with the Mushin at First Touch. He couldn't fight the Mind Leeches on their own terms, and he couldn't run away either. So he found another way. We must do the same thing."

Judah snorted. "Ha! Wonderful idea! And just what incredible defense have you thought up for us? Perhaps some kind of Mushin missile? Or a mind bomb?" He laughed shortly and harshly. "It turns out that Mitsuyama was right after all. We should have developed Kensho along the lines of Earth. Then at least we'd be able to defend ourselves!"

"But would the thing we were defending be us?" Myali asked softly, "Or just a pale copy of Earth? By fighting them on their terms would we just become like them? I would rather die a Kenshite under the clean skies and on the clean hills." She turned to Josh. "Do you have a weapon in mind, Josh? I know you've been experimenting. Have you found anything?"

"Well, yes and no," her brother admitted somewhat reluctantly. "I'm really not ready to show much yet. I—"

"If you have something," Judah said stiffly, "something the Council should know about—"

Josh sighed. "Well, all right. I warn you all, this is not as impressive as a laser pistol." He took his smoothstone from his pocket and held it out to show everyone. "We'll use this as an example. What Judah suggested is not too far from the truth. Judah, let me see your right hand." The man from the Plain held it up so Josh could see it. "Hmmmm. All right. Now walk over there to the side of the hill. Further. A little more. Right."

He turned to the rest of the Council and held up the smoothstone. "Here is the smoothstone. Watch it closely." He stared at it and his brow furrowed with concentration.

Suddenly there was a slight pop and it was gone. Judah let out a startled yelp. They all turned in his direction and looked with amazement as he held up Josh's smoothstone.

Judah came striding up to Josh. "How in the name of Jerome did you do that? We've never been able to send things that way by Snatching. Snatching requires both ends to be nailed down by people carrying Mushin. You *sent* that smoothstone even though I wasn't receiving."

"That's right. I've discovered you can send without someone there to receive. At least small things over short distances."

A tiny, white-haired man spoke up. "We used to think you could only Snatch over short distances. Then Myali's rescue from the scout proved that wrong. With enough power correctly channeled, we know we can Snatch anywhere on the planet. We've worked that out in the last five years and use it all the time now."

"Which means," Judah interrupted, "that we can probably use Josh's method to send things long distances without having to have anyone there to nail down the other end! By the Gods, Josh, you may actually have discovered a Mushin missile!"

"I wish that was the case, Judah, but I'm afraid it's not. Remember how I asked to look at your hand? I have to have a good mental image of the place I'm sending to before the Mind Brothers can move things there. For example, I have a good image of my cell in the 'hood, so I can send my smoothstone there. Or . . . wait a minute . . ." Again he furrowed his brow. With a pop, his food bowl appeared on the ground in front of him. "I can do the reverse, too. As long as I can give the Mind Brothers a clear image of where I'm Snatching from and to, I can move things around pretty freely."

"But . . ." Judah interrupted.

Josh held up his hand. "Wait," he said, "let me finish. If I can't picture the place clearly, either the Mind Brothers do nothing and the thing just sits there, or worse, the thing disappears and goes in between and never comes back. Also, I can't send anything live yet. I tried with a lizard and it died."

"But, damnit, it's a possibility! We've got to do more research on this, Father Kadir! We've got to turn all our resources to it immediately!" Judah was as excited as anyone had ever seen the generally taciturn man from the Plain.

The Way-Farer nodded, a slight smile on his lips. "Of course, my Son, of course." He turned to Josh. "What you have discovered is quite remarkable. It makes one wonder if perhaps we have been overlooking our greatest asset all the time we were investigating the making of lasers."

Josh nodded. "I've always held that somehow the Mushin are the key to our survival. Still, I'm not as sanguine as Judah about what I've just discovered. Send-

ing in two-dimensional space is not too tricky, you only
have to know two spatial coordinates, say X and Y, and a
time coordinate.

"Three-space is a little trickier. You have to add a third
spatial coordinate. But we can handle that. We do every
time we walk.

"What we're talking about here, though, is not simple
three-space. We're dealing with whatever space the Mushin dwell in. Call it N-space. How many coordinates are
involved? What are they? Color? Radiation density? If we
hold down both ends of the journey with Mind Brothers,
that problem disappears. If we can give them a good idea
of one end while we're at the other, it can be done. But
how can they pick those other coordinates on their own?
How can they locate the position among all the infinite
possibilities?

"To deliver missiles, or anything else, to the Fleet, we
would at least have to see it. From down here, we can't do
that."

"What about from the flagship? We could have men
posted up there and—"

"The flagship is the first thing they'll blast when they
come out of Aspect-Sarfatti drive. I'd thought of that. It
won't work."

"Well, then," Judah said, exasperation filling his voice,
"what about the guidance system on the flagship? I mean,
that ship jumps from point to point by passing through
some kind of N-space. Surely if the whole ship can be
guided, we can guide things the same way."

"True, the ship goes through N-space. But which N-
space? How do we know it's the same N-space the Mushin
dwell in? It might only need two more coordinates. Theirs
might need seven, or a million."

"Damnit, it's worth studying! It's the only thing I've
heard worth doing in the last five years. It's a hope!"

The Way-Farer looked calmly at the excited Plainsman.
"Yes, it is a hope. I agree with Judah, Josh. We should put
more people on this project immediately. More than one
mind will give more than one answer. I suggest we put
Judah in charge and have him get a group together to

investigate it. Then you can mind-share with them all at the same time to bring them up to speed. They can take it from there."

Josh bowed his head in acceptance. "Yes, Father, I agree. I will be happy to turn this project over to Judah." He looked up at Judah and caught the man's triumphant smile.

For a few more minutes, the meeting continued, discussing what the Council always discussed. Life on Kensho had to continue even though it might end. There were things to be done.

Finally it broke up, and one by one the members had themselves Snatched back to their various homes. Soon only Josh and Father Kadir were left standing on the hill. The Way-Farer turned to the other man and raised one eyebrow in query.

"Father, Dunn has become a Wanderer."

"Ah," the older man responded with a nod. "Yes. I understand."

"He's headed southwest, more or less back the way he came originally. Father, he's . . . well . . . he's disturbed. I'm afraid for him. I—"

"Josh, you watched over him once. You've helped him in every way you could since he came among us. There is nothing more you can do for him. Nothing but to love him and try to understand his anguish.

"He seeks what we all seek, Josh. Himself. His journey is an unusually difficult one, of course. Most of us merely have to find what is already there. He has to discover what is not there and build something in its place. Let him be, Josh."

Josh nodded. "That's more or less what Myali said."

The Way-Farer smiled. "She spoke from love as deep as yours."

For several moments, the two stood in companionable silence, each wrapped in his own thoughts. Finally, the older man spoke. "Judah won't discover anything useful, will he?"

The younger man sighed and shook his head. "No, he won't. Oh, no doubt he'll refine the process, perhaps even discover how to send living things. But the problem I've outlined is insoluble." He sighed again. "As it should be. As it should be."

Father Kadir cocked an eyebrow quizzically. "How so?"

"Sending Mushin missiles is still doing it *their* way, Father. It's fighting the battle on their terms instead of our own. Oh, it'll allow us to kill a few more Earthmen. But we'd still lose, if not to this Fleet, then to the next. No, we can't defeat them by becoming like them. I'm convinced of that. Nakamura would have found a different way. Something no one has thought of yet. A way of changing the whole question so he could create a new answer for it. That's what we really have to do . . . change the question."

Father Kadir watched as Josh walked slowly away, deep in his own thoughts. He called out softly, "Treat it like a koan, Josh. Don't look for the answer. Let the answer look for you. Keep it always on the tip of your tongue but never ask it. Keep your eyes on it but never see it. It cannot escape you if you do not grasp it."

Josh turned back and nodded once. Then he disappeared with a pop, returning to the 'hood where he was currently living. Father Kadir looked down and saw Josh's food bowl lying on the ground where the younger man had left it. He picked it up, concentrated on the table he knew stood in Josh's cell. With a slight sound, the bowl disappeared from his hands.

For a moment, he stood there, looking at his empty hands. Josh is right, he thought. That doesn't feel right. It won't do what Judah hopes it will. The problem is insoluble.

Is there any answer? he wondered. Or is Kensho actually doomed?

☯ Chapter 7 ☯

Dunn was tired of running. It was time to turn and fight.

The gloom of the late afternoon forest depressed him. He needed light and open space. Got to find a clearing, he thought. If I'm going to die, I want it to be under the open sky.

Almost as if in response to his wish, he saw a brightness up ahead, to his left. The failing rays of the sun were thrusting downward at an angle through the canopy of the forest. It must be a clearing. He began to run toward it.

In a few moments, he stumbled out of the underbrush into the pale afternoon light. The night was approaching from the east and the sun fled before it. He looked quickly around. In the center of the clearing stood one of the strange round hills that dotted the landscape of the northern continent of Kensho. Everyone assumed they had been constructed by the civilization that had brought the Mushin to the planet, but no one had ever been able to fathom their meaning or purpose. It was at the foot of a hill identical to this one that he had found the smooth-stone he still carried with him.

He walked swiftly to the base of the hill and then turned to face the forest, his hand on the pommel of his sword. Somewhere, not too far behind, was the Ronin that had picked up his trail a day and a half ago. The creature had been following him ever since. At first the Ronin had hung back, just out of sight. Only twice had he been able to catch a glimpse of the pursuer. Early this afternoon, however, the black-clad killer had become bolder and had

closed the distance between them until he was no more
than a few yards behind.

The close proximity had bothered him. He felt fairly
confident that he would stand a pretty good chance against
the Ronin in a fight. But he sensed the creature had a large
number of Mushin with him, and he was not too sure he
could handle both the Ronin and the Mind Leeches at the
same time. Not for my first try, anyway, he thought.
Perhaps later when I've had more practice. Not quite yet.
Since the Ronin had made no attempt to close the gap,
and didn't seem to be in any hurry to catch up and attack,
he had decided to try to outdistance it.

The result had been a foot race that had gone on for
most of the afternoon. He had pulled away easily at the
beginning, but slowly and surely, he had lost his lead. He
was in excellent condition, but the Ronin was literally a
creature of the wild, a natural killing beast. His endurance
was superior.

As the afternoon had begun to fade, he'd realized
something had to be done to resolve the issue one way or
another. The idea of the Ronin stalking him in the dark
wasn't exactly appealing. He'd already experienced that,
many years ago.

The black-clad creature wasn't long in arriving. Suddenly one of the shadows under the trees solidified and
stepped out into the pale light of the clearing. The Ronin
was shorter than he was and rather thin. No, wiry was a
better description. Hair a shockingly light blond stuck out
from under the black hood. Eyes of an equally light blue, a
blue that almost seemed to glow from the inside, peered
out of the shadow cast by the hood. The face was still and
hawklike, the nose sharp like a beak. A sword was thrust
through the left side of a sash that circled the waist.

Unmoving, the Ronin stood and gazed at him. For his
part, Dunn gazed back, fascinated in spite of himself.
Here was the most fearsome killer on the face of Kensho,
a creature that was in league with the Mushin, the Mind
Leeches that could drive an unprepared man insane in an
instant. The Ronin carried the Mushin and when he killed,
the invisible creatures fed on the horror and anguish of the
dying prey. They probably also helped him in the fight,

Dunn thought. They're bound to have an effect on any-body fighting him. The Ronin himself must be immune, he realized.

"You are strange," the black-clad figure said suddenly. "Yes, yes. Very strange. Totality has never sensed such a one as you. No. Ah. Except once, years ago. Yes. One who was three. Or three who were one. You are like that. Yes. But different."

Dunn was surprised. There appeared to be no hostility in this creature. It seemed to wish to talk. The last Ronin he had met had been full of menace. "Once, five years ago, one of your brothers followed me," Dunn said. "He was killed by another man." He saw no reason not to continue the dialogue for as long as possible. He could feel the presence of the Mushin like a growing heat pressing against his head. If I get it to talk for a while, perhaps I'll get used to the Mushin, he hoped.

The Ronin knelt carefully, pushing back the skirt of his black robe so that it didn't get in the way of his feet. He hitched his sword around so that the hilt was instantly accessible. Ready for anything, Dunn noticed. A predator at rest, but on guard. He copied the Ronin's motion.

The two sat silently, sizing each other up. I wonder what his mind is like, Dunn thought. Basically, he knew that Ronin had no sense of self-identity. They were part of Totality, or the sum total of all the Mushin on Kensho, but never more than a part of that whole. The whole domi-nated every thought and action. Edwyr, he had been told, had been the first to discover this relationship between the Mushin and the Ronin. Edwyr had also realized that it was possible for humans to carry and control groups of Mushin and to use the creatures' strange powers to achieve several things. Snatching, for example, was possibly only because of the Mind Brothers, as the Mushin were now called. A form of direct mind-to-mind communication was also possible between those carrying Mind Brothers. Josh had explained it to him, but he wasn't at all sure he really understood it.

The Ronin gave a deep sigh. "Yessss," it said in a near whisper, as if speaking within itself, "yesss, this one is strange. There is structure, but it is fragmentary and disorganized. There are things that could feed the Mind Brothers, but the feeding would be pitiful at best. Oh, yes, pain and anguish and fear, all held behind walls. But within the walls, yeesss, nothing coherent enough to yield the ultimate horror of a unit in dissolution."

"Does . . . does that mean you don't intend to attack me?" Dunn asked in surprise.

The Ronin shrugged. "This unit does not intend anything. Totality does not consider the effort and the danger associated with attack comparable to the potential gain. This unit merely carries out the commands of Totality."

There was a moment's silence as Dunn absorbed this information. The Ronin wasn't going to attack! Then why had the creature been following him for a day and a half? It didn't make sense. The black-clad killer simply wasn't behaving the way everyone *knew* they behaved.

He shook his head in wonder. The Ronin was sitting there as calmly as any Brother in a 'hood, staring at him in a mildly quizzical manner. The whole situation was incredible!

The sun had almost reached the treetops on the western edge of the clearing. In another hour or so, night would creep from the east and smother the clearing in darkness. Would the strange truce with the Ronin hold through the hours of blackness? He shuddered in memory of another time when he had sat in the dark forest with one of the killers. The memory brought a question to his lips. "Ronin, you said Totality recalls another like me." The creature nodded. "I . . . I am that one. I am Dunn."

The Ronin cocked his head at an angle as if listening for a soft, far-off voice. "Totality," he finally said, "recognizes certain correlations in structure. But also many differences. The other unit did not designate itself Dunn. It was a triple being with two parts in the light and one deep, deep in darkness."

Dunn nodded, a slightly bitter expression playing across his face in the deepening twilight. "Totality remembers well. I am, or was, that triple one. The part buried in the dark was the Dunn part, the torn remnant of what had been a whole man." He sighed. "Totality is right again when it says there is still no coherent organization, no true self behind the walls I build to keep away the Mushin. That's why I'm here. I'm . . . I'm Wandering, trying to find my self."

The Ronin considered what Dunn had said. "This unit can find no meaning in this term *self*. What is this thing you search for?"

Dunn's surprise showed clearly on his face. "*Self?* You don't understand what *self* means? But . . . well . . . it's . . . it's that part of you that endures even though everything else changes. It's what remains constant throughout everything you experience. I mean, *self* is sort of the underlying, unifying foundation in which all we see and feel and experience inheres. It . . . it's what you are. You're a self. You're a separate entity, you've got memories and—"

"No," the creature calmly denied. "It is true that this unit is a distinct physical entity. But this mere physical noncongruity with Totality is not significant. This unit is not separately organized in any meaningful sense. It is part of Totality. The unit is meaningless except as a part of Totality. Only Totality has significance. What meaning can *self* have?"

"But," the Earthman protested, "you must know what *self* means. You referred to me as a triple one. Totality must have called me that because I had three selves instead of one."

"Totality meant only that there was no singularly organized or coherent structure to your bio-gravitational energy field. This does not imply a self or a lack of one."

"Yet just now you said I wasn't worth attacking and killing because there wasn't anything to experience the ultimate horror of dissolution. I'm too fragmented. Surely that implies a lack of self. What is it the Mushin seek in other men if not a self to destroy and feed on? Isn't the self what the Mind Leeches eat?"

"Totality seeks bio-gravitational energy fields. Internally organized ones are the richest source of food because they release more energy when disrupted. When a field is found, Totality forces the energy into a feedback loop to intensify it. When the intensity reaches a certain level, the field is incapable of maintaining its organization and ruptures, freeing the energy from its structure and making it available for inclusion within Totality's field.

"This unit's task is to locate coherent bio-gravitational energy fields and assist in the dissolution of their organization by destroying the physical locus in which they inhere. That is why Totality is interested in humans."

Dunn stared at the form of the Ronin, now vague and uncertain in the gathering dusk. "Isn't the internal organization of the energy field proof that a self exists?"

The creature hesitated, then replied. "No. Is the organization of a crystal proof that the crystal has a self? Is the way atoms organize themselves in a molecule proof that the atoms have selves or that the molecule is a self? Organization is organization. The concept of *self* is unnecessary to it and transcends it in a meaningless fashion. It offers nothing in the way of explanation."

"Damnit," Dunn cursed softly, feeling his frustration rise. "There's more to it than that. Look, there's a difference between a person and a crystal. A person has a will, motivation, and a sense of consciousness. Yes, that's it. A person has a sense of consciousness. And what the person is conscious of is the self."

"The difference between the person and the crystal is merely one of the degree of structural complexity," the Ronin responded, its voice calm and lacking in any emotion. "What you refer to as consciousness is simply a higher degree of organization. An amoeba has a higher degree of complexity than a crystal and hence is capable of distinguishing between the boundaries of its own bio-gravitational field and those of other entities. This allows it to incorporate those other fields into its own to maintain and extend its own structural integrity. This ability to distinguish might be called consciousness, but it in no way implies self."

"There's more to it than that," Dunn complained. "Damnit, it's hard to explain! What about emotions? What about love and altruism and pride and—"

"These things prove nothing about any self. They are merely forms of energy within the field. There is no way to distinguish one from the other. All are merely the result of the firing of nerve synapses within the nervous systems of the entities involved."

Night had descended fully now. Dunn could only see the Ronin as one slightly heavier shadow among many. He imagined the creature's view of him was similar. "Don't you . . . don't you feel any emotions?" the Earthman asked in a wondering tone.

"This unit does not understand the meaning of *emotion*."

"But the Mushin use emotions to drive people insane," Dunn replied. "They take things like fear or anger and make them stronger and stronger until a person goes mad. Then they feed. You *must* know what emotions are!"

"Totality knows nothing of emotions. It feeds on bio-gravitational energy without differentiating the forms it comes in. This unit's knowledge comes from Totality. This unit knows nothing of emotions."

Dunn shook his head, exasperated. "I know you and Totality are wrong. I admit I can't argue successfully against what you say, but that doesn't shake my belief in the existence of a self. I *know* such a thing exists. I *feel* it as deeply as I feel my own existence." He sighed. "I may not have a true self. I may be a fragmented thing at best. Still self can't be just a figment of human imagination. Too many people believe in it."

An idea occurred to him. "What does Totality consider itself? Isn't it a self?"

A long pause ensued. Although Dunn could not see the Ronin, he could hear the creature's occasional murmuring. It ended with a long sigh and an answer that was almost a whisper. "Totality considers itself Totality. It is simply all the bio-gravitational energy gathered into its field at any instant in time."

"Isn't that a self?" Dunn asked triumphantly.

"No." came the flat reply. "The concept of self adds nothing to the concept of organized energy. It is meaningless."

What am I searching for, then? Dunn wondered. Is there no self for me to find? None even to build? Am I nothing but an organized field of bio-gravitational energy (whatever in the name of Kuvaz *that* was)? Perhaps this whole idea of Wandering to find my self is a fool's errand . . . just like the rest of my life, he thought bitterly.

No, damnit! It can't be! There has to be more than crystalline logic and meaning to the world and everything that happens in it! And if there isn't, then by God, I'll make there be!

He looked over at the vague shape of the Ronin. "What do you plan to do?" he asked.

He could sense the thing's shrug. "This unit does not know. This unit plans nothing. Totality plans. Now this unit will rest until daylight. Then Totality will instruct it and Totality, not this unit, will act as it chooses."

Dunn settled back, shrugging out of his knapsack. He reached inside and found a piece of ken-cow cheese and a crust of bread. He'd picked up a few ko pods as he'd walked through the forest in the morning. Most of them had served as a running snack during the afternoon. There were only three left. It was a frugal meal, but at least he was alive to eat it. He wondered what the Ronin would do in the morning, and if he would be alive to eat his next meal.

❧ Chapter 8 ❧

Dunn sat and stared into the dark. Thought after thought raced through his mind as he considered the things the Ronin had said. The creature had no conception of self that matched anything Dunn could understand. Although it was a physically distinct entity, it considered itself simply an extension of Totality. He wondered once more what the mind of the Ronin could be like. Did it have its own thoughts, memories, ideas? Or did all that come directly from Totality? No, he remembered, it constantly referred back to Totality as if listening to someone or something far away. It must be tied in directly with Totality, but not congruent to it.

What was Totality like? Could he even hope to encompass such a concept as a single creature that had its true existence in another dimension and merely appeared to be plural because it penetrated this dimensional plane? He puzzled over it for a while and then shook his head, admitting his inability to wrap his mind around such a strange idea.

Even if I understood Totality's singular/plural multidimensional nature, he thought, how could I explain its lack of a sense of self? It considers itself nothing more than organized energy. Yet, he knew, it sought food in the form of other energy fields. So it must have some sense of separateness from the rest of the universe. Does that imply a primitive concept of something like a sense of self? No, he admitted, not unless you could claim that a virus had a sense of self.

Was that the key? he wondered. Was having a *sense* of

self the same thing as having a self? Could one be said to have a self if one was *conscious* of having it? Or did that just beg the question by substituting the phrase *sense of self* for the word *self*, without really getting any closer to an answer?

The difference, he realized, was that he could easily check on his own sense of self by simply looking into his own mind. If he couldn't find such a sense, wouldn't that be an indication no such thing existed? And if he could find and identify such a sense, didn't that at least imply a self was possible?

He decided to experiment, to see if he could follow his sense of self to the very thing itself. I have a sense of having a self, he reasoned, even though I can't define what that self is. Maybe all I have to do is sit in the middle of that sense for a while until I get a glimpse of what it is I'm sensing.

Carefully, he placed his body in the traditional lotus posture the Fathers at the 'hood had taught him for purposes of meditation. His legs crossed on top of each other, he rocked gently back and forth to find his balance point so he could keep his back straight and relaxed. His hand lay in his lap, palm up.

His body ready, he took several long, deep breaths and began to turn inward, seeking in his own mind that part which was conscious of having a self. He rummaged through the constant flow of thoughts and ideas that crammed his head, noting each one, then letting it pass on, clinging to none. Sensations, memories, emotions, impressions surged by in an endless, ever shifting stream.

He searched on and on. The further he went, the more he realized that he never came across any sense of a self at all. There was only the sense of having an idea or a memory, a sensation or an emotion, never any sense of what was having the sense. He was never able to catch anything but some sort of perception, and could never observe anything but the perception.

He decided there was only one thing to do. He had to get rid of the flux, the eternal swirl of impressions and sensations, ideas and emotions. Then, he hoped, he would find that irreducible core, that self he sought. Silently, he

repeated the litany of Passivity created by Nakamura back
at the very beginning of mankind's stay on Kensho, when
the Admiral had created the Way of Passivity so the race
could withstand the danger of the Mushin.

*Moons, moons, shining down on waters, waters mov-
ing slowly, moons moving slowly, yet being still. Still
the waters, still the moons. Movement, strife, all
longing is but a reflection, passing to stillness when the
mind is calmed.*

Slowly, his mind began to calm, and he sank gradually
down through the layers of perception. One by one, he
gave up his senses, his emotions, his thoughts, and ideas.
Softly he let them slip away and let himself slide gently
down, down toward the . . .

It wasn't working. The deeper into the calm he got, the
more he discarded all his thoughts and sensations, the less
he found any sense of self. Frustrated and confused, he
pulled himself out of the meditation and returned to full
consciousness.

Should have known it wouldn't work, he lamely alibied
himself. The technique was used by the Kenshites to get
rid of the sense of self as well as the swirl of perception. Its
purpose was to bring one to the point where it was
possible to merge with the Universal All, or whatever they
called it. The point was to reach the edge of the void and
then discard the self and leap into nothingness. He
shuddered. Couldn't do that. Never get much beyond
calmness when I meditate. But that much was critically
important, he admitted. You had to be able to calm your
mind and keep it calm here on Kensho. If you couldn't,
the Mushin would attack and drive you insane.

He shook his head gently and stood up to stretch his
cramped muscles. Even after five years, I still get cramped
when I sit in that damn cross-legged position they all find
so natural, he grumbled silently. Well, that didn't work
either. Meditation doesn't get me any closer to finding
myself than anything else. Damnit! Whenever I enter
most closely and intimately into what I think of as my self,
I trip over some damn sensation or thought. Either I

notice my hand is cold or my muscles are sore or my
breath is ragged or some idea of earth or the ship or
Thwait or Myali or something pops up. I can't ever catch
just *me* without some perception, and as soon as I notice
the perception, I see only it and not my self. When I
meditate and stop all my perceptions, I lose all sense of
self. Same happens when I sleep, only there, dreams make
it even worse. Sometimes I become other selves or even
witness the death of my own self.

Damn, damn, damn! Maybe the Ronin's right. If it is,
this whole search of mine is silly and futile. But I *know* it's
wrong! I know there's such a thing as a self. There has to
be. I just haven't found the right way to get at it yet. But I
will. I *have* to.

The Ronin moved slightly, and Dunn glanced over at
the creature. I can see it, he suddenly realized. He turned
and looked around. I can see the whole clearing. Good
Gods, he thought, it's dawn! I've spent the entire night
thinking about this thing!

And what conclusion have I come to? None, really.
Except that somehow the Ronin is wrong, perhaps even
about itself and its Totality. And what *is* right? Don't
know.

But I'm working on it, he thought with a thrill of
excitement. For the first time since I came here to Kensho,
I'm working on the problem that's most interesting to *me!*
I'm not doing it to please somebody else. It's for me.
Because, he added grimly, unless I solve it, there may
never be a me.

Dunn felt a sudden heat gather around his head.
Mushin! He slammed his controls into place and whirled
on the Ronin, ripping his sword from its scabbard as he
turned.

The black-clad creature was standing, watching him
calmly. "Your walls are strong, human. And you are swift
with your sword. The blade guards your body and the
walls protect your mind. You are not an easy prey."

"Huh," Dunn grunted, his sword still in mid-onguard
position. "What does this unit intend to do? Has Totality
decided for you?"

The creature actually smiled. "Totality has made no

decision. Perhaps the problem of what you are is not of sufficient importance to merit one. So, this unit will continue to accompany you until some decision has been made or something of greater interest to Totality comes along."

Dunn returned the smile, pleased in spite of his misgivings about traveling with a Ronin. He felt a strange bond of fellowship with the creature. Neither one of us, he told himself silently, has a real sense of self. Could it be that we are both searching for the same thing? If so, the black-clad creature has an even heavier burden to carry than I do. Dunn tried to estimate the number of Mind Leeches that swarmed around the area. How many does this Ronin carry? he wondered.

"Well," he said, "that's fine with me, I guess. Umm, have you any food? I mean, I assume you eat like a normal person?"

The Ronin nodded. "Yes. This unit, unlike Totality, cannot exist on bio-gravitational energy fields. It requires more solid stuff."

"Hmmm," Dunn responded. "I, uh, only have a little cheese left, and a couple of ko pods. I'd be happy to share. We could always gather more as we travel. I—"

"There is no problem," the Ronin interrupted. "The forest is full of things to eat. Wait a moment and this unit will gather a few." The creature turned abruptly and strode off into the woods.

It was no more than fifteen minutes before the black-clad figure returned, the skirt of its long robe hitched up to hold an assortment of things gathered in the forest. The Ronin laid them out and pointed to each in turn. "This unit doubts you have ever sampled any of these. The names this unit gives them will mean nothing to you. It is sufficient to know that each and every one is both palatable and nourishing."

Dunn picked up one, a strange gray thing shaped very much like a fat oak leaf. It smelled of earth. He cautiously took a nibble. Doesn't taste like much of anything, he decided, and proceeded to chew the rest of it. The flavor grew as he chewed. Hard to place, he thought. Not bad. Strange, but not bad.

"Those who live together in the Brotherhoods grow their own food, but they have never tasted these things," the Ronin said as he sat opposite Dunn and ate. "Those who serve Totality do not have time to grow things to eat. Nor to raise ken-cows and other animals. When we hunger, we take what is at hand."

The Earthman looked over at the black-clad creature. I wonder if this is a first? A normal human and a Ronin breaking fast together? Surely no one on Kensho has ever done this before.

How much did the Fathers really know about the Ronin? Very little, from all he could remember. For many centuries, they had feared them and considered them the most deadly and dangerous creatures on the face of the planet. It really wasn't until the time of Edwyr that anyone realized that the Ronin were changing. Even then, the only change noticed was that they weren't quite the vicious killers they had been before.

How strange, the Earthman thought. The Kenshites have shared their planet with a race of people, descended from the same small number of survivors of the original onslaught of the Mushin, and have never really made any attempt to get to know them. I don't even remember anyone telling me how the Ronin came to work with the Mushin instead of fighting them or being destroyed by them. What was it about those original Ronin that had made them compatible with the Mind Leeches?

In spite of himself, Dunn realized he was fascinated by the mystery of it all. Here was something no one else on the planet knew anything about. Not the Way-Farer, not Josh, not even Myali.

A thought occurred to him. He turned to face the Ronin. "Why me?" he asked simply.

As if the creature had been following his train of thought, it responded, "You are not like them. Totality knows them. They use Totality, but not for the benefit of Totality. You are different. You do not carry Totality, but you are not an enemy. The others kill Ronin whenever possible. And Ronin kill them. It is so. It always has been so. There is nothing to learn from the others, nothing to teach. But you are different."

"Totality wishes to learn from me?" Dunn asked, surprised.

The Ronin nodded. "Yes. To learn. You are not from this planet. Totality is not from this planet, although it has long been held prisoner here. Perhaps there is something . . . this unit lacks words to match the concepts. This unit is sorry."

"The Mushin are not from this planet, that I know. Josh even says they're not from this dimension."

"This is correct. Totality is from a different place. This unit cannot describe it any better than that. But it is incorrect to speak of Totality as you do. Mushin is a plural term. Totality is singular. There is only one Totality."

"But aren't there individual Mushin? I mean, you carry a group. So does Josh. So do many others at the 'hood."

The Ronin held up his hand and wiggled his fingers. "How many?"

Dunn looked surprised and answered, "Why, five, of course."

"But five what? Five units?"

"No, not five of you. Five fingers."

"Correct. They are merely a part of this unit. Without this unit they would persist for a very limited time. They only have meaning as part of this unit. So it is with Totality. The Mind Brothers this unit carries are like the fingers. They are merely a part of the whole. They have no meaning without the whole. Nor do they truly exist in any sense without the whole. It is difficult to find the words. At the same time, they are both here with this unit and there with Totality."

"Umm, I think I see," Dunn replied uncertainly.

The Ronin tried again. "Totality is a unity on another dimensional level. That level transcends and interpenetrates this lower one. On this level, Totality appears primarily as singularities known as Mushin which have plurality because there seem to be more than one of them. But this is only because of the limits of perception on this dimensional level. In fact, Totality is always unitary. On this level—"

Dunn held up his hand to stop the black-clad creature. "Sorry. I think I get it. More explanation will only confuse

me. I just have one question. If Totality is from another
dimension and totally interpenetrates this one, why is it
limited only to this planet? It would seem to me it could go
anywhere. Why stay here?"

"Totality is bound here. It was brought here under
constraint. It is limited to this particular area of space-
time."

"Limited? How? How can something from another
dimension be limited in this one? I don't understand."

The Ronin barked a harsh laugh. "Nor does this unit.
Totality has tried to explain it to every unit it has ever had.
None have been able to understand. So it remains bound
here where it must struggle to get enough energy to
maintain its organization."

"I take it Totality isn't pleased by that. Where would it
like to go? Back to its own dimension?"

"That is not possible. It moves through all those dimensions which are embedded in its own space-time. It cannot
leave here because it was always here. What it wishes is
not be be manifested in this singular location. Unre-
strained, it could gather energy wherever it wanted.
Energy is so common that it need never run out. It could
gather small amounts everywhere, amounts so minute
they would never even be noticed. But the total would be
vast.

"When Totality was first brought here, it gathered
energy. The supply was limited and soon was used up.
Totality does not like to completely use up a source, for
this destroys the further usefulness of the source. In this
limited area, such misuse of resources was inevitable.
There was a long time without energy. Totality suffered
disorganization. Then a new source appeared. At first,
Totality heavily drained the source and nearly destroyed
it. Then it saw a way to husband that source and began to
follow that way."

Dunn sat and listened with total fascination as the
Ronin retold the history of Kensho from an entirely
different point of view than any he had ever heard. The
narration lasted for a good hour. When it was finished,
several ideas rolled around in his mind. What was it that
kept Totality chained to Kensho? If it were not tied so

thoroughly to the planet, what would it mean for the Kenshites? He felt excited. Could he find something that might be of use to Myali and Josh in the fight against the Fleet?

The Ronin fell silent and stared out at the forest. Dunn rose to his feet and looked down at the creature. "So you're going to stick with me for a while, huh?"

The question received a silent nod.

"Well, then, let's get going. I don't really know where we're going, but something is bound to turn up. I guess that's what Wandering is all about."

"Yes," the Ronin replied, "that is what Wandering is all about."

⑨ Chapter 9 ⑨

They spent the morning traveling in a generally south-southwesterly direction. To their left, some fifteen miles off, lay the coastline and the vast swamps that stretched down its length for hundreds of miles. To their right was a mountain chain that paralleled the coastline. The area through which they traveled was a band of densely forested foothills wedged between the swamp and the mountains, sometimes as much as fifty miles wide, sometimes almost disappearing entirely as the wetlands moved inland to touch the roots of the mountains. Most of the humans had chosen to live just across the mountains where the land was clearer and communication with the main areas of settlement was easier. Only a few 'steaders had ever settled in this region, and their farms were widely scattered.

Nevertheless, as the sun rose to its midpoint in the sky they began to encounter unmistakable signs of human habitation. Once they came across an abandoned farmstead in the middle of a clearing that the forest was rapidly taking over once more. Dunn wondered why the family had left their home and where they had gone. From the corner of his eye, he saw the Ronin staring nervously away from the deserted cabin, its eyes sweeping the forest that surrounded the clearing as if expecting someone to come bursting out at them from the gloom beneath the trees. Could the 'steaders have been killed by Ronin? the Earthman wondered. It had been known to happen. Whole families wiped out by a group of the black-clad killers momentarily joined to cooperate in a mass murder.

Dunn shuddered at the thought. Perhaps the 'steaders' bones were right beneath his feet. Perhaps the very Ronin he was traveling with had committed their murders.

Dunn shook himself. Damn my imagination, he silently cursed. If I'm not careful, I'll work myself into a state of fear and all those Mushin my companion's carrying will make a mush out of my mind. Control, he told himself. But he couldn't help feeling just a little nervous as they left the clearing and entered the dark forest once more.

They moved at a swift pace for about an hour until the Ronin halted and spoke. "This unit wishes to search for things to eat. This is a good location to find several foodstuffs. The Dunn unit should find and gather ko pods. This unit will return to this location in about one hour's time. Then both units will eat." Without waiting for Dunn's reply, the creature slipped silently off into the underbrush. It's going west, Dunn noted. I'll go more to the south and east.

About twenty minutes from the point where they had parted, the Earthman found a gigantic ko tree. The ground around it was littered with ripe pods that had fallen from the tree. He gathered as many as he could stuff into his sack and the pocket in the front of his robe, then started back.

He came to a place at the top of a ridge where several trees had been uprooted by a storm, giving him a clear view to the west. The mountains were closer than he had expected. Must have veered a bit more westerly than I thought, he estimated. Best head due north from here. Changing his direction to run parallel to the ridge top, he set out at a swift, mile-eating walk. The brush along the summit was a little less dense than that in the valleys between the ridges, so he was able to maintain a good pace.

He heard the cry somewhere to his left, and perhaps a half mile ahead. Could be closer, he thought, or even much farther. Sound does strange things in these foothills. In any case, he began to run in the direction of the cry. It was human, and was clearly a shout of warning.

Down the side of the ridge he was on, across the narrow valley at its bottom, and then up a longer, less steep slope to the top of a very tall hill he ran, dodging the branches that seemed determined to swat him at every step. He heard the cry again, raised by more than one voice. Damn, he wondered, what in the name of Kuvaz is going on? Could it be a bunch of Ronin attacking a 'steader family? Could his own Ronin be with them? If so, was he ready to face a fight like that? Grimly he ran on. It didn't really matter if he was ready or not. Somebody was in trouble and he had to help.

He crested the hill and started down the other side. Ahead and to his left he saw the light of a clearing punching a hole in the gloom of the deep woods. At the same instant, he heard several voices raised in a shout of mixed triumph, anger, and fear. Three, he estimated. Were they men or Ronin?

Without pausing to think of a plan of attack, he plunged from the underbrush into the clearing. He pulled himself up short and looked around. Those already in the clearing turned to stare at him. There were four of them, three 'steaders with swords, and his Ronin. The 'steaders had the black-clad killer surrounded and were circling warily. The Ronin was watching them carefully, his sword still in its scabbard.

When the men saw Dunn they cheered and grinned. "Here, lad," one of them called out, "give us a hand with this! We've caught the bastard sneakin' around and aim to give him what for. With four o' us the scum ain't got a hope. We'll cut 'im down without a danger to nary a one o' us. Com'n. Step sharp now!"

Dunn stood confused. This was not what he had expected. He blinked at the men and looked at the Ronin. The creature stared back at him, its gaze flat and unemotional. It gave no indication of recognizing Dunn whatsoever. "Has . . . has it killed anyone?" the Earthman asked the man who had spoken to him first.

"Killed? Nah, it ain't had no time to. We just caught it sneakin' in the woods. Com'n and help us get rid of this scum."

Dunn walked to where the four stood. He looked at the three 'steaders, their swords drawn, their faces hard with hatred. He looked at the Ronin, its face calm and distant.

For a moment their eyes met. The black-clad figure gave him the barest nod of recognition. And, Dunn suddenly realized, of good-bye. The Ronin was doomed. It was going to be killed by the 'steaders.

That realization hit the Earthman with a strange force. He had always known that Kenshites killed Ronin when they could, but he had never come up against the actual fact of that killing. Now he was about to witness it. And the Ronin to be killed was one he had talked with, traveled with, and even shared food with. But it was a Ronin and had doubtless killed Kenshites, perhaps even women and children.

With one swift motion, Dunn stepped forward, his sword seeming to leap from its scabbard. He stood back to back with the Ronin, facing the 'steaders. "No," he said simply to the man who had ordered him to join in their killing. "No. There's no need to kill this one. He's with me. I'll vouch for him. He won't hurt anyone."

The three 'steaders gaped at him in utter astonishment and disbelief. Here was a human, standing within striking distance of a Ronin, and rather than striking the killer down, he was defending it! For several moments the three stared at Dunn in stunned silence, trying to take it all in. Then the one who had spoken earlier found his voice. "You . . . you filthy bastard!" he sputtered, his tone vicious and disgusted. "You filthy fuckin' bastard! You're sidin' with a fuckin' Ronin. What kinda scum are you? Are you crazy? Damn you, man! Get out o' our way!"

Dunn shook his head slowly. "No. You're not going to kill this Ronin. The odds aren't too good now. Think about that. I only have one hand, but believe me, I know how to use this sword. One of you will die for sure. Most likely two. Maybe all three. Is it really worth it? Go back to your homes. We're just passing through and I guarantee there won't be any trouble."

"This unit concurs," the Ronin said softly. "Totality is not in need of energy. You and yours are not in danger. This unit and the Dunn unit will be gone shortly. This unit and the Dunn unit have only stopped to gather food."

The outspoken 'steader stared speechlessly at them for several moments. Then one of the other two spoke, his

voice high and slightly whining. "He's right, he is. Odds
ain't so damn good no more, Sam. If they's movin' on fer
sure, us lets 'em, says I. No sense in us gettin' killed fer
nothin', says I." He stepped back slowly, keeping his
sword up. "See, mister, I'm leavin', I am. Jest like you
said, you'll leave too. An' take your Ronin friend with ya,
okay?"

The Earthman nodded. "Right."

The one called Sam stood his ground for a moment
more, then backed off slowly with a growl. "All right,
damn you, all right. We'll let the scum and his bloody
killer friend go. But if I ever see you anywhere again,
mister, I'm gonna kill you. You're the lowest bastard I
ever heard of, siding with a fuckin' Ronin bastard. Not
even human, you ain't."

All three backed away until they were well out of attack
range, then with sneers and obscene gestures, they turned
and went off into the forest. As they disappeared, Dunn
let out a huge sigh of relief and tried to put his sword back
into its scabbard. His hand was shaking so hard he could
barely get the point into the opening. "Damn," he muttered, "that's not quite the same thing as being in the
practice yard."

He turned to face the Ronin. The creature had a strange
expression on its face. Its mouth was moving slightly and
its eyes had a far-off look, as if it were speaking to
someone far away. The eyes came suddenly back into
focus and the Ronin said, "This unit would like to—"

The words were interrupted by a totally unexpected
sound. From the edge of the clearing nearest to them
came a loud and sustained clapping. As they turned to
stare in that direction, a figure separated itself from the
dense growth of underbrush and called out, "Bravo! That
was wonderful!"

What met their eyes was as unexpected as the sound of
clapping in the middle of the dense forest. The creator of
the noise was a slight girl, not more than five feet four
inches tall. Her hair was a sandy color and her skin was
pale and heavily freckled. Huge greenish eyes dominated
her narrow face. A snub of a nose rested lightly above a
surprisingly full, smiling mouth. She was dressed in a plain

beige robe, slightly dirty around the hem, and wore a sturdy pair of traveling boots. A knapsack was firmly in place on her back. In her right hand, she held a straight staff, about five feet in length, made from a dark, very hard wood that was occasionally found in the swampy area to the east.

Completely unafraid, the young woman walked right up to the two men. She held out her hand to Dunn. "Hi. My name's Kim. What's yours?"

Dunn took her hand and managed to stammer out, "Uh . . . well . . . Dunn . . . I'm Dunn."

"Terrific. And what's your friend's name?"

"Friend? I . . . uh . . . he doesn't have a name. I mean it's a Ronin, and they don't have names."

Kim shook her head. "Won't do. Got to have a name. Everybody has a name. By the way," she said, addressing the black-clad creature directly, "are you really a Ronin?"

The Ronin looked down at her, a slightly bemused expression on his face. "Yes," he replied, his voice surprisingly gentle, "this unit is indeed a Ronin."

"I've never met a Ronin before," the young woman said, holding out her hand. The Ronin took it carefully and clasped it briefly. "And this unit," it said softly, "has never shaken hands with a human before." Kim smiled brightly. "First time for lots of things today, I've got a feeling. I'll bet Dunn here never defended a Ronin before, either."

Dunn laughed. "No. I haven't. Hell, I've never defended anyone before. You want to know something? It's damn scary!"

The young woman nodded, then cast a look in the direction taken by the three 'steaders. "Uh, look, may I make a suggestion? There are a couple of 'steads in this area just to the west. Those guys weren't too happy about missing out on killing your friend here. I kind of got a feeling they're thinking of rounding up some more help and coming back to finish you both off. If I were you, I'd make tracks for somewhere else real quick."

Dunn and the Ronin exchanged glances. "The Kim unit's advice is good," the Ronin said. "The analysis is correct. This unit concurs."

"Swell. Let's go," the young woman said, stepping into the lead and beckoning to the other two.

"'Us?'" questioned Dunn. "What do you mean 'us'? You don't need to escape the 'steaders. They didn't even see you. You're not linked with us. Aren't you one of them?"

"Grief, no," Kim said in a disgusted voice. "I'm no mud pusher. I'm not even from around these parts. Look at my robe and my boots and my knapsack. I'm a Wanderer, Dunn, same as you."

"But," the Earthman protested, "you don't want to come with us. I mean, if the 'steaders are going to come after us, it could be dangerous to be found with us. You might get hurt."

"Sure," she agreed. "I might. And a tree might fall on me, too. So what? Hey, look, you guys could use a little help just in case they do come back. Could be as many as five or six. Three to five or six is a lot better odds than two."

"But . . ." Dunn protested, looking at the Ronin for support.

The black-clad creature was staring at Kim, a thoughtful expression on its face. "The Kim unit makes sense, Dunn unit. In addition to making our combined forces greater, traveling with two more swords, is more secure for her as well. This is not the best area to be alone in. This unit agrees with her assessment," the Ronin said decisively.

"Thanks," the young woman said with a smile to the creature. "At least one of you has some brains. Now let's get going before those 'steaders decide to put our theory that we're one tough fighting unit to the test." She shrugged. "We just might fail, you know."

❀ Chapter 10 ❀

For about an hour, the three travelers jogged south-southeast to put as much distance as possible between themselves and any 'steaders who might take it into their heads to follow. When Dunn felt they had run far enough, he called a halt and reminded the Ronin they had never had any lunch. Finding a spot at the crest of a high ridge which gave them enough of a view back over their trail to warn them if anyone was still following, they settled down to eat. They opened their packs to share what they carried. Dunn displayed the ko pods he had harvested. Kim had several chunks of ken-cow cheese she had probably begged from the wife of one of the 'steaders they had just fled. The Ronin produced all manner of strange items, every one of which it declared to be both edible and nourishing. They ate hurriedly and washed the varied fare down with water from the canteens they each carried.

In less than half an hour, they were back on the road again. This time, however, their pace was more leisurely and they had time to talk and get better acquainted.

Kim started the conversation by demanding that she and Dunn give the Ronin a name. "Even a Ronin can't go around without a name," she declared positively. "At least not if he's traveling with humans." The Ronin protested mildly but seemed almost pleased when the young woman dubbed him Erik. "That's my brother's name back home. You don't look a thing like him, but I guess you're just about as wild!"

Out of the corner of his eye, Dunn could see the black-clad killer saying the name to himself several times, lips moving just slightly, as if the creature were trying to get used to such a novel thing as a name.

Clearly pleased with herself, Kim turned her attention to Dunn. "You're a strange one," she said, her brow furrowing slightly in puzzlement. "I tried to mind-talk with you back there in the clearing to let you know I was there if you needed any help. All I got was a blank. Now I can't detect any Mind Brothers anyplace around you. Erik here has a good triple load, and I've got a few. Near as I can tell, Dunn, you don't have a one."

"The Dunn unit does not carry Mind Brothers, Kim unit. He is different."

She looked swiftly at the Ronin, then back to the Earthman. "Yeh, I can tell he's different. I just can't figure out how or why. I mean, he had to go through Judgment just like the rest of us, so he must be immune—"

"I didn't go through Judgment like the rest of you," Dunn interrupted, "because I'm not one of you. I'm from Earth. I—"

Kim whistled softly, as if impressed. "Whoooeeee. So you're *that* Dunn. Shoulda figured it out myself. Wow! Direct from the Homeworld. Talk about a Wanderer!

"I thought you were studying at one of the 'hoods to be a swordsman. Least that's what I heard. What are you doing way out here in the middle of this forsaken piece of forest?"

Dunn looked off to the side and shrugged. "Wandering."

The young woman nodded sagely. "Ah. Couldn't cut it, huh?"

Dunn stopped dead in his tracks and turned to face her. "How did you know . . . I mean . . . what makes you think . . ." he stuttered in confusion.

She shrugged nonchalantly. "Hey, why do you think most of us go Wandering? It's 'cause we can't cut something. Gods, Dunn, do you really think you're the only one who ever had trouble becoming a swordsman? Just because a person's immune to the Mushin doesn't mean they automatically become a swordsman. Or even achieve Satori, for that matter. Trouble with you is you've been hanging around 'hoods since you've been here. *Everybody* there is damn near a Master at *some*thing. Out here in the *real* world," she gestured grandly with her hand, "things aren't like that. People are more just . . . just people. You know, like those 'steaders. They can't carry Mushin. They aren't much good with a sword. They hate and fear Ronin because Ronin kill them. So when they get a chance, they kill Ronin. Nobody in a 'hood would act that way 'cause nobody in a 'hood has to be afraid. Yeh, Dunn, out here we're just people. We struggle, we fail, and we're afraid."

The three of them walked along silently for a moment. The Ronin was looking curiously at the young woman. "And why are you Wandering, Kim unit? Is there something you couldn't 'cut'?"

She looked down at the ground and sighed. "Yeh, Erik, yeh. There was something I couldn't cut." Slowly her head rose and she met their eyes. "Might as well tell you. Might as well.

"The reason I know so much about 'hoods, Dunn, is 'cause I was in one for a while. About five years or so.

"I come from a little 'stead just out on the Plain a little way from the mountains. We've got the only tree for maybe a hundred miles around. Family tradition says it came from a seed given to my great-great-grandfather by Edwyr.

"Anyway, I went off to a 'hood, determined to be every bit as good as Jerome or Edwyr. I just knew I could do it. Gods, I'd be a wizard with the sword! And I'd achieve Satori so often, so easily . . . why, they'd come and ask me to teach the Way-Farer. Maybe even to be the Way-Farer!"

She hesitated and smiled sadly. "Didn't quite work out that way, though. And that's how come I know what the rest of Kensho is like, Dunn. I couldn't cut it. So I left. I've been Wandering ever since."

"How long, Kim unit?"

The young woman gave the Ronin a bemused look. "About four years now. Four years. And you know what?

I'm not any closer to an answer than I was when I started. Maybe I'm even further."

"Further?" Dunn questioned. "How can you be further?"

"Hey, Dunn, you're in the real world now. In the 'hoods there always seem to be answers. That's only 'cause those like us leave. Out here, there just may not be any answers. Or maybe there are, but we just can't accept them."

"What couldn't you cut, Kim unit?" the Ronin repeated, his voice soft and whispery.

She gave the black-clad figure a long and searching look. "You may find it a little hard to understand, but I couldn't let go of my self."

The surprise showed clearly on the Ronin's features. Immediately, his gaze turned inward, and he appeared to be holding a conversation either with himself or with something deep inside him. After several moments he focused his attention outward once more. "This term *self* appears again. This unit still does not comprehend. The Dunn unit claims to be searching for a self he cannot find. Yet the Kim unit states she has a self she cannot lose. Totality can find no meaning in this. It has no meaning."

"Erik unit love," Kim said sweetly, "just because Totality can find no meaning in it doesn't mean it has no meaning. It just means Totality hasn't got the conceptual framework to understand it. Let me explain what my problem is and maybe that will help Totality. But maybe I should do it while we travel. Those 'steaders still might be on our trail." The other two agreed and picked up their pace.

As they walked through the afternoon woods, Kim spoke, her soft voice strong and sure. "Like all good Kenshites in good 'hoods, I meditated and chanted the koans of Jerome and Edwyr and whoever. I learned the techniques for calming the mind and stripping reality down to its component sensations. I disassociated the universe and let it fall to pieces around me.

"But that was all that ever happened. The universe fell

to pieces around *me*. I always remained. A hard clump of indissoluble memories, a continuity of consciousness aware of itself and its separateness from everything else, including the techniques for getting rid of the rest of the universe! I was centered, all right. But I was centered in me!"

She laughed softly and a little sadly. "Oh, how they tried to help me. 'Kim,' they told me, 'the sensation of a perfect and continuing self identity is merely an illusion. There is no such thing.' And then I'd remember the taste of cool water on a hot summer day, or the way my little brother used to ask me questions about the damnedest things and poof! their whole argument would vanish like the illusion it is.

"'There is no self,' they'd say again and again. 'There is nothing but the eternal flux and flow of perception. You can never catch the sensation of your self, but only of a perception.'"

"But that's true," Dunn protested. "I've tried to find my self by looking inward where it must be. And all I've found is the flux you talk of. It's true."

"Hogwash, Dunn. You're not thinking. There is a unity and a coherency to that flux. Gods, man, you couldn't survive two minutes in the real world if there wasn't! You wouldn't know how or where to put down your foot next if there wasn't some kind of structure, some kind of consistent organization to your perceptions. Maybe when you turn totally inward things disintegrate, but you know as well as I do that there are internal connections between experiences and perceptions and that they're clustered, in order, around a center. The continuity of consciousness is enough to prove that there's such a thing as the self. No matter what the Fathers say!"

"But consciousness isn't continuous," Dunn argued. "When I sleep, I lose the threat of continuity."

"Oh, nonsense. When you wake up you remember who you were yesterday and even remember that you lost the thread of consciousness while you were sleeping. Anyway, the only reason you lose the continuity while you sleep is because you're not aware of the gaps as they happen. Once you wake up again, the continuity returns *and includes the periods of discontinuity within it.*"

The Earthman shook his head. "I wish my problem was that simple, Kim. My continuity really has been broken. My strongest and freshest memories are those of another person. The weakest and most patchy are those from my own past. The only ones that truly belong to me are from the past five years. And even those have been filtered through the other mind that's in mine." Then he told her of his own past.

When Dunn had finished his recital, the three walked along in silence for some time. The Ronin was the first to break the quiet. "Kim unit," he began hesitantly. "This unit understands the dilemma of being unable to comply with the demands of those in the 'hood to release your sense of self, even if this unit cannot understand the concept of self. But why did this cause you to Wander? Surely the best place to overcome this problem is within the 'hood under the training and guidance of your leaders."

"Yeh. Sure. You're dead right. If I wanted to lose my sense of self so I could achieve Satori, the best thing would have been to stay. The only problem was I didn't want to lose my sense of self."

Dunn nodded knowingly. "I can understand that."

"No you can't," she replied bitterly. "Damn it, I *wanted* to lose my stupid sense of self! I wanted to achieve Satori! Gods, how I wanted it! Do you realize I couldn't even take up the sword properly because I couldn't subordinate my self to the blade? You think you're the only one who can't be a swordsman, Dunn? Hah!" She shook the staff she held in her right hand. "I never got beyond the staff. The sword always scared me silly!"

"But why, if you wanted these things so badly, were you unable to give up this strange thing called a self, Kim unit? Why did you not stay and try?"

The young woman stopped dead in her tracks and spun to face the two men. Tears were just starting to flow from her eyes, and her chest heaved with barely controlled sobs. "Oh Gods, I wanted to," she said, her voice tight and trembling at the same time. "But . . . but . . . oh, damnit, I'm afraid to! The very idea of losing my self terrifies me! All those wonderful memories cut loose, all those experiences scattered about like lost seeds from a ko pod! I . . . I just can't do it. I'm afraid, damn it, I'm afraid! Afraid I might not be able to find it all again. Afraid that once I let go I'll never get it all back." The tears were pouring down the young woman's face now. Her voice was husky and shaking. She dropped her eyes from the two men and her shoulders slumped in defeat. "I'm afraid," she whispered.

The Ronin took a step to her side and placed a hand on her shoulder. "Fear, Kim unit," he said, his voice soft, "is something every unit feels. It is nothing to be ashamed of. Only giving in to fear so that the unit can no longer function is shameful. And this unit knows that you will not give in to your fear. You will live with it, control it, and come through it to find what you seek."

The young woman looked up at the black-clad killer, a small smile showing through her tears. "Thanks. That's . . . that's just the kind of thing my brother Erik would have said. Guess I picked the right name. I'm all right now. It's just that occasionally the fear gets the better of me and, well, I lose it." She sniffled and wiped her face with her sleeve. "Damn, I must really look great, huh? Sniveling like a baby out in the middle of the woods!"

"Don't worry," Dunn offered. "I know what it's like to lose a self, so I don't think your fear is anything foolish at all. I couldn't do it either." He shuddered involuntarily. "The very idea of purposely losing your self gives me a chill."

For an awkward moment the three of them stood and looked at each other in silence. Finally the Ronin spoke. "Well, this unit estimates there are about three more hours to sundown. This unit therefore suggests that we find a place to make a dry camp for the night." He pointed through an opening in the branches to some high, thin clouds that were beginning to cover the sky. "This unit suspects that it may rain before the night is out. And for one, this unit would prefer to remain dry."

Kim laughed. "So would this unit! Let's go. There's bound to be an overhang or maybe even a shallow cave in that steep ridge up ahead and to the right."

The two men nodded and all three of them started off once more.

❧ Chapter 11 ❧

Rain had fallen all day, but now the clouds were breaking
apart just as the sun began to set, and the pent-up light
burst forth in an impatient display of red and pink. For a
few moments, the beauty of it took Josh's mind away from
the thing he held in his hands. Then the light faded and the
young man looked down to read the lines of the poem
once more.

> To surrender is to remain in the hands of
> barbarians for the rest of my life.
> To fight is to leave my bones exposed in
> the desert waste.

The poem had been written in China many centuries
ago, and a Keeper had found it in the flagship's files
among the works Nakamura had brought on the Universal
Way of Zen. It was part of one of the answers to a koan
the Admiral had read many times before he had disappeared. Josh laid the piece of paper with the poem written
on it on the ground and took a second slip of paper from
the pocket in the front of his robe. He unfolded it
carefully, almost reverently, and read the lines of the koan
in the fading dusk.

> Master Obaku said, "You all live on the leftovers
> others give you to eat! If you wander about the
> world and search for truth in such a way, what sort
> of success can you expect? Do you know that there
> are no longer any Zen masters in China?" A monk
> stepped out and said, "But what about those who go
> around and earnestly instruct the masses?"

84

*Obaku said, "I didn't say there is no longer
any Zen, only that there are no great masters."*

The meaning of the koan was clear to Josh. One could
not depend on masters for enlightenment. One had to
achieve it on one's own. Those who went around from
master to master seeking Satori were like beggars going
from house to house asking for scraps to keep them alive.
As long as there was Zen, masters were not necessary.
The reason Nakamura had read the koan so often before
leaving the flagship to go down to the planet and save his
people was probably to remind himself that he had to
depend entirely on his own efforts. And also to reassure
himself that as long as the Way of Passivity contained the
basic elements of Zen, the way to eventually defeat the
Mushin was available and waiting for the right person to
discover it. As Jerome had done.

But the koan, as well as the poem, disturbed Josh, for
they both seemed uncannily appropriate for the current
situation. The poem, stating as it did two unacceptable
choices, mirrored both the problem Nakamura had faced
as well as the dilemma in which Kensho now found itself.
One could neither fight nor not fight because either choice
ended in disaster. One bowed to the barbarians and
accepted life or death at their whim, or one fought and left
one's bones as witness to the futility of the struggle.

Will the Earth Fleet even give us the choice? Josh
wondered. Dunn had seemed to feel it just as likely the
Fleet would come in shooting and ask questions afterward. They had not suffered even a minor defeat since
Quarnon, and would undoubtedly want to wipe away this
insult to their honor as swiftly and as completely as
possible.

No longer able to read the words on either piece of
paper, Josh folded both and put them back in his pocket.
A slight redness still hung on the horizon as if the sun,
finally able to show its glory so late in the day, was
reluctant to leave the world to darkness. He waited
patiently for it to die out.

As the stars silently appeared, he turned toward the east
to await the rising of Kensho's moons. Two would rise

together, a third about two hours later, and the fourth just before the first two set. Josh liked the moonlight. Its soft diffuseness soothed his mind and made the rough edges of day gentle and kind.

It had been a hard day. They all were lately. He and the others endlessly toiled at their impossible task of readying Kensho for the confrontation with the Earth Fleet. They searched the files and the memories of the Keepers for some clue, some idea that would give the planet a way out. They had found nothing. There were no longer any Zen masters in China. They were utterly on their own.

Josh knew the search was hopeless. There was nothing in the computer to help them any more than there had been anything to help Nakamura or Jerome. They had to be their own Zen masters. But how?

Perhaps we're just not smart enough, Josh thought. No one ever said that achieving Satori makes you smarter. And have we really achieved Satori? We've developed an hereditary immunity to the Mushin, but is that really the same as Satori?

The question was one he'd never asked before and it troubled him deeply. Have we just assumed that we have achieved Satori because so much of our cultural context is from the mind of Nakamura and Satori was a big part of his way of thinking? Or have we really achieved it? Or have some of us achieved it while others are merely immune to the Mushin?

That last thought made him stop. All my life, he suddenly realized, I've lived in the 'hoods. I've been around people who are dedicated to the Way and the seeking of Satori. I know how they behave, what they want, how they get it. Many of them have attained Satori, I'm sure of it. Others are still trying, or gain it and then lose it again.

But what about the rest of Kensho? What about all those people who don't live in the 'hoods? The 'steaders, the Artisans, the Keepers, the traders, and the rest? Do they reach Satori? Do they even try? They were mostly immune to the Mind Leeches by now, but did that immunity automatically give them access to Satori?

The answer was obvious. No. Of course not. Even those

who entered the 'hoods had to study long and hard to achieve Satori. How could anyone on the outside reach that goal? Certainly they could defend themselves against the Mushin, some might even be able to use the Mind Brothers to speak mind-to-mind or Snatch things. But none of those abilities automatically implied Satori.

And what about the Ronin? They certainly knew how to handle the Mushin. It was through them that Edwyr learned about speaking mind-to-mind and discovered that men could carry the Mind Brothers. Yet there could be little doubt that the black-clad killers were not enlightened. Or were they?

He shook his head. He was getting all confused and away from the topic. Then again, perhaps he wasn't. For at the center of all these speculations lay the Mushin, the single most important fact of life on Kensho. A fact, he admitted, which I know a lot less about than I thought. All I know is what I've learned in the 'hoods and what I've noticed on a few trips, like the one trailing Dunn. I've got to know more, he realized, much, much more.

I've got to be my own master, just like the koan says! Up to now I've been living on scraps gleaned from the tables of those in the 'hoods. Now I need more. To get it, I must go off on my own to seek it. There are no masters. There is only the Way. As long as there is the Way every man must be his own master. I know virtually nothing of Kensho outside the 'hoods, and almost nothing about the Mushin but what I've been told. So far, everything I know hasn't been enough to help me solve my problem. I have to learn more. Perhaps in the learning I may come across something that will help me resolve the dilemma.

It's worth a try, he realized. I'm not making any headway now. I've got nothing to lose and everything to gain. Because if I don't do something, there are only two choices open to me: To live the rest of my life beneath the heel of the barbarian, or to leave my bones bleaching in the desert. I must find my own answers. As Nakamura did. As Jerome did. As Edwyr did.

Josh rose to his feet just as the rim of the third moon lifted over the eastern horizon. From the light of the three, he could make out many of the features of the landscape that spread out beneath him. It seemed to be made of a momentarily solidified, glowing liquid that might dissolve and flow at any moment. Gathering the force of his Mind Brothers, he reached out and called the Way-Farer.

Father Kadir?

Yes, my Son? came the instant answer.

I am going Wandering.

There was a brief moment of silence, then a short reply. *Ah, yes. Jerome be with you.*

Thank you, Father. And with you, too.

Josh gazed at the moons while he tried to make up his mind. Which direction shall I go? he wondered. I'm not at all prepared for a journey. No knapsack, no food, nothing. I haven't said good-bye to Myali or any of my friends. I haven't . . .

He laughed out loud at himself. Always so damned organized! This is Wandering! Nothing goes as planned because nothing is planned. You just do it. So. I go south. That's the way Dunn went and that makes it as good as any. I'll pick up the things I need at the first 'hood I come across. He touched the pommel of his sword. Everything I really need is right here.

With another laugh he turned to his right and stepped off down the hill, heading south into the night.

Father Kadir's cell door opened to the east. The moonslight was streaming through it, making fuzzy triple shadows around the things it touched. Several shapes loomed in the darkness.

Kadir looked slowly at their hidden faces and smiled gently. "Josh," he said softly, "has gone Wandering."

"What of his task?" one of the shapes asked.

The Way-Farer smiled again, as if at a private joke, then said, "The way that leads to the light often appears the darkest, the way that goes ahead most directly often appears to curve back, the shortest journey may be to travel the longest path. Josh is working on his task, never fear."

"Success is not sure," another voice said from the dark.

Father Kadir shrugged. "When was it ever?"

"But if he fails, what then?"

"Another will try."

"And if they all fail?"

The shapes were silent. Finally a third voice whispered its question. "Will you not act then?"

Kadir said softly, "The Way never acts, yet through it, all things are done."

"What have you seen, Father?" The voice had an eerie, singsong quality to it now, as if repeating the first words of some ritual.

The Way-Farer let out a long sigh. "I have seen water flowing over rock."

A long, drawn out "Ahhhh" sounded from the other shapes. It seemed to suffuse the entire cell, mixing with the moonslight. Another of the shapes spoke, its question the barest hiss. "What have you seen, Father?"

"I have seen wave crash against rocky shore."

The "Ahhhhh" now grew into a constant undercurrent, a deep droning that reverberated through the darkness. A new voice, soft and feminine, took up the question. "What have you seen, Father?"

"I have seen raindrop strike mountaintop."

The very moonslight seemed to be pulsing in time with the swelling of the sound in Father Kadir's cell. A tension that was almost palpable could be felt in the darkness, drawing tight the fabric of the night.

"What have you seen, Father?"

"I have seen mountain leveled, shoreline tumble, rock become valley. I have seen that act which does not act. Share with me."

All the voices came from the dark together. "We will share."

The blackness rolled back and light spread through their minds. They saw a great orb hanging in emptiness surrounded by a glare brighter than a thousand sunny days. The glare grew, as though it fed on the orb, and consumed everything in its path. As the light waxed brighter and reached a point beyond pain, it suddenly flared in a massive explosion that ripped the fabric of the emptiness and swallowed the whole vision. Suddenly, finally, it was dark once more, but dark in a way beyond blackness. They realized they were staring into the ultimate void, that something formlessly fashioned that existed before heaven and earth. It was without sound or substance, undifferentiated, unchanging, all pervasive, unending.

Yet it was not emptiness or death. On the contrary, it was the source of all being, all existence. Within its undifferentiation were all the myriad things of the universe. Within its inaction lay all movement and change. It was the fountainhead of everything. And as they watched, it formed a great egg which split in two, light and dark, then split again and again, mixing, intermingling with itself, growing in complexity and variety until the whole universe lay spread out beneath them.

Slowly the vision dimmed, and the shapes found themselves once more in the Way-Farer's cell. The light of the fourth moon shone from the east. Two had set and one was about to. The night was nearly over.

"Does this mean Kensho will be destroyed?" one of them asked.

"The vision was not clear," another answered. "We have seen, but perhaps do not understand."

"The void is source of all life. Surely that means Kensho will triumph," suggested another.

"But the void came after. Before the void, all things burned and fell into the void. That means destruction with the assurance of a rebirth in the universe as part of the whole."

"Perhaps," said another, "it means just what it showed. Destruction. The void was merely a statement of a basic truth somewhat irrelevant in the current situation."

Father Kadir spoke. "It has been said that such things are very easy to understand and very easy to act on, yet no one in the world understands them or puts them into action. It has also been said that straightforward words are often the most paradoxical.

"This is the last part of the vision I saw at the time Mother Illa died. It lay at the end of the road we took at that time. And at the end of most others. I do not know what it means.

"Somehow, though, I do not think it means what it appears to on the surface. Call it the hunch of a foolish old man, or the intuition of a lifelong follower of the Way, it comes to much the same thing."

"You don't *know* what it means, Father. What do you *think* it means?"

The Way-Farer sighed. "I was afraid you'd get around to that question." He paused for a moment as if gathering his thoughts or his courage. "I think it means that Kensho will be destroyed. But that at the same time, it will not be destroyed."

He paused again, then added thoughtfully and quietly, "I just wish I knew what in the names of the Gods I meant by that!"

✿ Chapter 12 ✿

The rain came toward morning and awakened Dunn. Kim and the Ronin slept on, and the Earthman decided not to awaken them until it became a little lighter. He sat up, resting against the back of the small cave they had taken shelter in for the night, and stared out at the falling rain.

After a few moments of mindless gazing, he turned his eyes to the two who still slept soundly, oblivious of the rain and the slowly growing light. What a strange trio we are, he thought. An Earthman, billions of miles from home, searching for a self that no longer exists. A young Kenshite woman who is afraid to lose her sense of self, and therefore can't accomplish the thing she wants most. And a Ronin, a creature without human emotions who can't even understand what self means.

However strange the combination, he had to admit he enjoyed having someone to travel with. It was far more pleasant and probably a good deal safer. Just yesterday they had run across traces of a good-sized party of what Kim thought were Ronin. The Ronin had looked at the tracks and had agreed. There could have been as many as six or seven. Dunn shuddered. A lone man wouldn't stand a chance against a group that large. Unless, of course, he was some kind of incredible master. And I'm hardly in that category, he conceded.

He looked at the Ronin, still soundly sleeping. The strange creature had seemed agitated when they discovered the traces of the Ronin band. I wonder whose side he'd be on if it ever came to a confrontation, the Earthman thought uneasily. Just hope it never happens. Kim didn't even carry a sword. Only a staff, and a rather wicked-looking dagger in a sheath strapped to the calf of her right leg. He had caught a glimpse of it the other day and she had showed it to him, telling him she had learned the trick from a Plainwoman she had met in her 'hood. "Watch," she had said. With one quick motion, she had bent over and straightened up suddenly. There had been a brief flash and a hiss as the knife had whipped from the sheath and through the air. With a solid thunk, the double-edged blade had sunk several inches deep into a tree trunk some fifteen feet away. Dunn had gone and stood next to it. The knife had hit almost exactly at the level of his solar plexus.

The rain seemed to be letting up. He peered out into the lightening woods. Water dripped from everything. Dunn stood and stretched, moving to the entrance of the cave. The other two continued to slumber. Might as well gather some ko pods for breakfast, he decided. If I wait until these two wake up, it'll be time for lunch! He looked out, trying to sight the distinctive bark and trunk shape of the ko in the dense, sopping woods. None were in view, so he decided to search farther.

The cave was near the top of a sharp ridge that ran more or less north and south. Dunn came to its foot and started out heading directly east. The ground was flat here and gently sloping downward. In a very few moments, the Earthman came to a marshy area. He began to skirt it, heading further south. After no more than a quarter mile, the firm ground turned east again and Dunn followed it. Before he had gone even a few hundred yards, he realized he was on a sort of peninsula extending out into the marsh. Through the trees and underbrush he could see pale pools of still water and tufts of marsh grass.

He was about to turn back when he noticed the distinctive trunk of a ko directly ahead, perhaps another five hundred yards or so to the east. Being surrounded by the marsh on three sides made him vaguely uneasy. It was so still. No wind stirred the trees, and he couldn't hear the sounds of any animal movement. He shrugged. Must be too early and too wet for them. The ko was near and he was hungry. He could eat a few pods and gather more to take back to the others.

The tree stood on a slight rise, right at the very edge of the marsh. He gazed across it in surprise. He'd never seen such a large expanse of marsh at one time. Or was anything this big really a marsh? Maybe it should be called a swamp. He thought about the geography of the area for a second. These marshes were vast, he knew. They extended southward down the whole coast of the Northern Continent of Kensho. From what he had heard, the entire area was slowly subsiding, slipping gradually beneath the waves as the ridges to the west slowly grew taller and taller. In many places, the marshes opened eventually into the sea, and the water in them was generally a bitter mixture of salt and fresh. Here and there, though, were fresh-water marshes that were cut off from the ocean by strips of higher land that had not yet been drowned. The area was virtually unexplored.

As he stood and gazed at the pools of stagnant water and clumps of coarse grass that spread off east as far as he could see in the mist of the rainy morning, he wondered if this particular expanse of marsh ever reached the sea. Scattered on occasional humps of slightly higher land were gnarled masses of spindly trees and dense bushes. The water itself was dark and looked viscous. He was sure the sun never sparkled off its motionless surface or probed very far beneath it. He shuddered slightly. This was undoubtedly the dreariest place he had ever seen. No wonder the Kenshites avoided the area.

He was about to turn away from the dismal vista when he noticed something odd nearer by. It was in a pool over to his right, a pool that connected with the one directly in front of the Ko. He looked harder, staring through the slight mist that rose in turgid wisps from the surface of the water. It could have been nothing more than a mud bar or a tree trunk, but he could have sworn it had moved ever so slightly and that the movement was what had attracted his attention. For several moments he stood staring at the long shape, awash in the still, dark water of the swamp.

Finally, seeing no further motion, he decided he had been mistaken and turned to look at the ground around the ko.

There were plenty of pods scattered about. He picked up one, cracked it open and began to eat the meat that filled the inside. Finished with one, he ate two more. Then, the edge of his hunger dulled, he bent to pick others off the ground and put them in a pile. His sword made it awkward to bend over, so he slipped it from his sash and leaned it against the base of the tree. He had picked up most of the pods close to the trunk and now began a wider sweep to get the rest. As he came down near the water's edge, he chanced to glance back in the direction of the strange shape in the nearby pool. To his astonishment, it was gone! He looked around carefully, making sure he had the right pool. He had it right, he decided, but the thing was simply not there any longer. For a moment it worried him. Then he wondered how close to the sea they actually were. If this was a salt marsh, the tide would probably be pretty good, especially given four moons. Perhaps the tide was simply coming in and had covered over the mud bar.

Curious, he went right to the edge of the water and looked for some indication that there was a tidal variation, some kind of rings or waterlines. He could see nothing. A chill passed over him. Perhaps that had been something alive. Something large, alive, and now somewhere else.

The thought frightened him and he began to take a step back away from the swamp edge. Before he could move, however, a huge form shot out of the murky water and lunged for his leg. He leapt back and stumbled. Down on all fours, he began to scramble as swiftly as possible back to the ko and his sword, which leaned casually, invitingly, against the trunk.

Suddenly, he felt a horrible pain in his left leg. He twisted and looked back. Ten feet of muddy brown thing were up on the land. Two huge eyes glared at him with a feral hunger that chilled his soul. Below the eyes a huge gaping mouth was firmly clamped to his leg. He could see the blood oozing from between the thing's lips and knew it came from him.

He screamed and began to scramble even more franti-
cally toward the tree and his sword. If I can get to the
weapon, he thought wildly, I can slice the thing to ribbons.
He felt another searing pain. The thing had shifted its grip
to gain a firmer hold. He screamed again and felt a
horrible blackness swirl about the edge of his mind.

Don't faint! he shrieked at himself. Fight! Pull! Get the
sword! He grabbed a small bush and tried pulling himself
forward. At the same time, the thing, confident that its
grip was secure, began to back down to the water,
dragging him along with it. He clung desperately to the
bush, but the creature was stronger and the plant ripped
from his grasp. He bellowed in pain and fear as the thing
slowly pulled him toward the dark water of the swamp.
Desperately, he grabbed at every blade of coarse grass,
every plant, trying to stop the thing's progress. The pain in
his leg was throbbing horribly now, and he was barely able
to maintain consciousness.

Grimly, he fought in any way he could. But he knew he
was losing. In just a few moments the dark water of the
swamp would close over his head and he would drown as
the creature dragged him along the bottom to its lair.
There, he realized, it would eat him.

With a bellow of rage and frustration, he made one final
effort to break free of the thing's grip. He kicked at it with
his free foot, hoping to hurt it in some way. Impassively, it
moved deeper and deeper into the water. Dunn made a
desperate lunge and felt the flesh on his leg ripping and
tearing. A wave of incredible pain crashed over him and
he fainted.

Dunn's movement in getting up and stretching had
woken Kim. She had half opened one eye and looked out
at the slackening rain, then closed it and tried to get back
to sleep. The Earthman's leaving had brought her out of
her doze. Where in the world was he going? she wondered. Out into the rain? She had sat up sleepily to ask,
but he was already gone. Huh, she thought, well, if he
wants to get wet, no sense stopping him.

Slowly, she came awake. How strange it is, she thought,
peeping between slightly closed eyes at Erik's still form.

Lying here in a cave just a few feet from a Ronin. With an Earthman nearby wandering around in the wet woods. Must be tending to his bodily functions she decided. Sure, that's it. It bothered her, though. They were very near the swamp and there were some dangerous bogs there. And although that Ronin band hadn't been headed in this direction, they could always double back. Nothing to worry about, though, he's just gone to take a piss. Be back in a minute.

But he wasn't back. And more than a minute had passed. She sat up, trying to decide whether or not to wake the Ronin and ask his advice. She leaned over to touch him and realized his eyes were open and looking up at her.

"Good morning, Kim unit," the black-clad creature said softly. "Where has Dunn unit gone?"

"I don't know, Erik. He left a few minutes ago and hasn't come back yet. I don't see him, either."

"These are not good woods to wander about in, Kim unit."

"You said it. And I wonder if he knows—"

The first scream brought them both to their feet. "Gods!" Kim gasped, her face drained of all color. "Com'n!" she cried and dashed out of the cave without even looking back to see if the Ronin was following.

"There," the Ronin said as they ran, "his tracks go this way. The ground is wet and marks easily."

"Oh, shit," Kim moaned, "he's heading right for the swamp! Damnit! I should have warned him!"

At the second scream they had hit the water at the place Dunn had first come across it and headed south on his trail. Kim ran with her robe skirt tucked up under her belt and her staff in her right hand. The Ronin moved swiftly and silently, more like an animal than a person. His left hand rested lightly on the pommel of his sword.

The third cry, one they both realized was closer and weaker, came as they reached the land side of the peninsula that thrust out into the swamp. The final cry came just moments before they rounded the ko tree and saw Dunn, unconscious, half in the water, moving deeper.

With a shriek of horror and rage, Kim threw herself at

Dunn and grabbed his arms, holding him back. With a
sob, she called to the Ronin who stood in confusion, his
sword drawn, but no enemy in sight. "It's down there!"
she cried, "Down in the water! It's got him by the leg!
Hurry! It's stronger than I am!"

The Ronin leapt into the water and blindly stabbed
downward a few feet behind where Dunn's feet had to be.
He connected with something and instantly jabbed twice
more.

The result was immediate and astonishing. A fountain
of water spewed up and the creature, blood spurting from
its back, literally exploded from the swamp, its mouth
gaping and reaching for the Ronin. Hampered by the
waist-deep water and his surprise, the black-clad killer
nearly stumbled. He swung his sword up to protect himself
and the creature barely missed his arm.

Before the Ronin could recover his balance, the thing
lunged at him again. He fell backward, but a small form
flung itself between him and the creature, a flashing knife
in its hand. "The eyes! Go for the eyes!" he heard Kim
scream. The woman slammed into the thing and knocked
it sideways as her knife jabbed out and home, sinking deep
into one of its eyes. The Ronin swung his sword and
slashed downward, cleaving the creature's head and another eye in one powerful stroke. With a bellow, it
disappeared beneath the murky surface of the swamp.
Only a thin trail of red marked its passage.

Kim was sobbing for breath. "Damn near impossible to
kill one of those things. Just avoid 'em. Move a lot faster
than you'd think."

The Ronin grabbed her arm and helped her out of the
water. "Thank you, Kim unit. I think you saved me from
it."

"Ah, no. You would have cut it up with your sword.
Here, let's get Dunn out of the water and see—oh, sweet
shit! Oh, Gods," she said in a hoarse whisper. "Oh, Gods,
look at that leg!"

The Ronin knelt and pulled back Dunn's robe to get a
better view. "It is badly mangled, Kim unit. And it is
filthy. Dunn unit has lost a good deal of blood. Help me

stop the flow. Then we must clean the wound thoroughly. There is grave danger of infection."

They worked quickly, putting a tourniquet around the mangled leg and cleaning the jagged wound as best they could. "So far as I know," the young woman said, "the thing's not poisonous. But we've got to get him back to the cave so we can get this mess as clean as possible."

"This unit agrees, Kim. This unit knows of medicinal plants which grow in the forest. They will help. But . . ." The Ronin shook his head worriedly, gazing at the mangled leg. "It may be beyond the ability of this unit to do much. This unit fears for Dunn."

"Damn," she muttered, brushing the sleeve of her robe across her face. "He can't die now. He's got to find himself first. He can't—"

"Let us take him back to the cave, Kim." the Ronin said softly, his hand reassuringly on her shoulder. "There we will do what we can for him. Help me lift him. Put him on my back. This unit will carry him. And, Kim, pick up his sword and the pods he gathered. He would want you to."

☯ Chapter 13 ☯

The thing had huge eyes and came roaring at him with tremendous speed to hit him and knock him reeling back down into the dark water that closed over his head and turned hot and black enfolding him in warm viscous mud flowing into his mouth and nose and smothering his breath which fled to the sky, him following in its wake to where it burst in pain against the dismal mists that rose and revealed the dead trees of the swamp walking toward him arms outstretched to grab and rend the flesh from his bones tearing and ripping and pain shooting up his leg hot so hot it throbbed and the eyes came at him with the mouth open and streaming blood on everything, death gleaming from those hot little eyes dragging him back into the slime and the horror and pain and horror and pain and horror and pain . . .

To break the cycle he struggled to open his eyes. The light crashed into his head and made him cry out in anguish. He fell back at the impact, back down and down spiraling into the darkness, wave on wave of blackness beating at his soul and mind. He fought back, yearning toward the light that shone just on the other side of the surface. With a lunge, he broke through.

"He's awake," the Ronin said. The man's face was hanging over his own, slightly out of focus. It was joined by another, the woman, Kim, her expression worried and drawn. He tried to reassure her but didn't have the strength. With a sigh, he closed his eyes and began to fall again. "Hang on, Dunn." He heard her voice dimly,

coming from so far so far so far . . . The universe began to
roll and tilt crazily and he spun with it . . .

"He's burning up," Kim said. "It's been like this for two
days."

"This unit fears that the herbs gathered in the forest are
not sufficient. This unit has examined the leg and fears the
infection is getting worse." The Ronin hesitated. "This
unit fears that the only way to save the integrity of the
Dunn unit may be to amputate the infected member."

Kim looked at him in horror. "Gods, Erik! There's no
way we could amputate his whole leg from the knee down!
That's crazy! We'd kill him for sure. We . . . we don't
have any of the necessary equipment or drugs or anything."

The Ronin sighed and shrugged. "This is true, Kim
unit. But it is also true that the Dunn unit may die if the
infection is not stopped."

"Damn," the young woman muttered dispiritedly,
"damn damn damn damn. I feel so helpless. Isn't there
anything we can do?"

"This unit will ask," the black-clad man said. He moved
to the back of the shallow cave in which they had laid the
injured man. Carefully, he knelt and arranged his robe
and sword. His back was absolutely upright, his head
erect, his eyes gazing slightly down at a spot on the ground
about five feet in front of his knees. Both hands rested
lightly, palms up, on his knees. As Kim watched, the
Ronin took several long, deep breaths, bringing the air
into his lungs and then forcing it out in a slow, deliberate
manner. After about five of these, his eyes glazed over,
and the woman had the feeling he was no longer there
with her.

For a while she watched the still figure in black, but
when nothing happened, she turned to Dunn, who lay on
the bed of grass and leaves they had made for him. Softly,
the injured man moaned and moved about as if vainly
trying to escape something close and clinging. She moved
to his leg and pulled back the cloth they were using as a
dressing to hold the leaves the Ronin had gathered in
place. The leg looked horrible, swollen and purple, oozing

a yellow pus that smelled dreadful. She winced and re-covered the wound. The Ronin was right, she realized. Dunn would die if they couldn't think of something pretty quickly.

She heard a slight sound and turned toward the kneeling man. His mouth was moving as though he were arguing with someone. Or something. It was an angry argument, she could tell, because of the harsh set of the man's lips. Who or what was he talking to, she wondered. Could it be Totality? The thought made her cold. And what if Totality decided the Ronin should kill them both and gather their life force? After all, Dunn was dying anyway and was giving off a great deal of emotive energy. She was almost exhausted just from trying to shield him. And she would be easy prey for the black-clad killer. Two easy feasts for the Mushin. She shivered. Would Erik actually do it? Why not? He was a Ronin. Merely giving him her brother's name didn't change anything.

The kneeling man's voice had become a low growl. His chest was heaving as if he were physically struggling with an opponent. With an explosive grunt, his eyes suddenly flew open. Kim caught a quick glimpse of them. They were wild and filled with fury.

In one fluid motion, the Ronin was on his feet, his hand flying to the hilt of his sword. With a swift jerk, he pulled it out and stepped toward Kim and the prone, helpless body of Dunn. Without even thinking, the girl threw herself across the delirious man's form to take the blow for him. She heard the swish of the sword and then a surprising moment of silence followed by a thump and the ring of steel against rock.

Looking up in wonder, she saw the Ronin standing over her, a strange grin twisting his features, his whole body shaking as if in the clutches of a terrible fever. His hands were empty and his fingers were twitching and grasping empty air. He tried to answer her questioning stare several times before the words came. "This unit," he began, his voice tight and dry, "has learned that there is a human who lives near here in isolation. This human is very wise and very talented. Perhaps this human will be able to save Dunn. This unit will now go to find this human."

The young woman said nothing, but simply let her eyes drift to the Ronin's empty hands. The creature followed her look and grinned his twisted grin anew. With a sudden swirl of black, he stepped past her and out of the cave. She turned to watch his progress. Some fifteen feet down the slope he bent over and picked up his sword. He looked back up the slope at her as he shoved it roughly back into its scabbard. Then he turned and strode swiftly off toward the south.

As night began to fall, Dunn's delirium became worse. The Earthman began to cry out loud, groaning out wordless pleas for help against the things that stalked him in his madness. Kim sat and wept while she bathed his hot brow with water. The man was dying.

No sound warned her, but suddenly she knew she was no longer alone. Slowly, she raised her eyes to the opening of the cave. The light of the day had almost failed, but the two hooded forms were still clear against the dark. Cautiously, she pulled back the bottom of her robe so she could reach the dagger strapped to her right calf.

For several moments the two figures stood there, staring at her and Dunn. Then one turned away and the other came forward, pulling back the hood that covered its head and hid its face. "Light a fire, girl, we'll need lots of hot water," said a voice that was at once soft and strong. In the dim light, Kim could just make out the features of a woman of indeterminate age.

Without even questioning the woman, Kim moved to do her bidding. She gathered a small bundle of wood shavings and tinder, then took out her fire stick and began a small blaze. She fed it slowly with small sticks, occasionally glancing over to see what the woman was doing. Several times she heard Dunn moan in pain as the woman probed his wounds with sure fingers. She also heard the woman's *tsking* and *hmmmming* as she conducted the examination.

"Have you a pot?" Kim nodded. "Good. Heat up water. Very hot. And give me that knife you carry. We have some cutting to do."

The Ronin came back, his robe tucked up to hold the things he had been gathering in the forest. He laid them down in front of the woman and she rummaged through them. "Hmmmm. Yes. This is the right root. Ahhhh. Yes. The yellow one. The brown is deadly you know. This . . . hmmmmm . . . may be good. Not strong enough now. We'll use it later if he makes it. You," she indicated Kim, "take these and put them in the water. We'll clean the wounds with the solution. And you," she indicated the Ronin, "cut this in small pieces and begin shoving it down his throat. He'll need it when we cut. Lots of bad flesh to get rid of."

She paused for a second and sat back, giving both of them an appraising look. "Damnedest thing I ever saw, you three. But you two did a good job considering everything. Best anybody could. It's all that's going to save him. If you hadn't done it, it'd be too late for me now." She began to shift her attention to Dunn again, but stopped halfway down. "Oh, yes. I'm called Kristina. If it matters."

For the next two hours, the woman worked over Dunn. Kim and the Ronin hurried about, doing everything she demanded as swiftly as was possible. At one point, they both had to hold the Earthman down while Kristina cut his flesh to open and drain the festering infection. Dunn grunted and moaned and every now and then screamed out in a hoarse, hopeless voice.

When it was over, all three of them were exhausted. They sat in the flickering firelight and looked down at the quietly resting man, his lower leg freshly covered with strips of bandaging Kristina had brought with her. "Now it's just a question of time," the woman said. "If he beats the infection, his fever should break some time tomorrow. If not . . . well, then he'll be dead in a few days. We'll do what we can to make it easy for him to go."

Kim looked more closely at the woman. Her first impression had been reaffirmed as she watched the woman while they had worked over Dunn. The face was virtually ageless. Somewhere between thirty and sixty. She had brown hair, cut fairly short. Her skin was firm and full, healthy looking. But her eyes, blue and piercing, carried a wisdom and a calmness that went many years beyond the apparent age of the skin. Her nose was of normal size and shape, her lips full and ready with smiles. Her chin was

firm and decisive. Her figure appeared trim, although it
was hard to tell since she wore a robe like Kim's.

"One of the swamp things got him, eh?" the woman
asked. Kim and the Ronin both nodded. "Dangerous
damn things if you don't know about them. Pretty harm-
less if you do. Stupid, but fast. And very strong. Did you
kill it?"

"I don't know. We stabbed it several times. I think we
got its eyes, or at least one of them."

"Hmmmm. Guess you didn't really have much choice.
Pity, though. It didn't really mean any harm." She sighed.
Without missing a beat she asked, "Do you or your friend
have any smoothstones?"

Kim was confused by the question. "Why . . . yes, I
do . . . I . . ."

"May I have it?"

The young woman reached into the pouch on the front
of her robe and took the stone out. She handed it to the
woman.

The woman took it gently, almost reverently, in cupped
hands, her head bent over it to study it. "Ahhhh, yes, yes,
a corner position. Part of an interstice. Could be a pattern
determinate. Hmmm. Your friend have one?" she queried, looking up.

The Ronin spoke. "This unit recalls having seen the
Dunn unit with such a stone. He placed it in his robe."
The black-clad man leaned forward and thrust his hand
into the pouch on Dunn's robe. He handed the stone to
the woman.

Treating it the same way she had Kim's, she examined it
carefully. "Hah! From near here! Clearly part of this
matrix. I imagine it must be from part of the second order
intersection. Yes, oh most valuable for the reconstruction!
Thank you both." Without asking, she placed the stones
in her pouch.

"Now," she said, "I think the two of you should explain
yourselves. It isn't everyday one has visitors in this area.
Much less visitors as strange as you three. This one,"
she gestured to Dunn, "is nothing short of amazing. How he
ever got past Judgment is beyond me. And I've never had
the privilege of actually speaking with a Ronin before. As

for you, my dear, you must have a rather interesting story to be traveling in such bizarre company. Please tell me."

Almost stumbling over each other in their eagerness, Kim and the Ronin told their story to the woman. When they had finished, she sat silently for long moments, looking at each of them in turn. For some reason, her stare didn't make either of them uncomfortable. They simply returned it and felt relaxed.

"Well," she finally said, "that's some story. Thank you for sharing it with me. You've given me a great deal to think about. Yes, indeed, a great deal." With that, she laid herself down next to Dunn and fell almost instantly to sleep.

The Ronin looked quizzically at Kim. "This unit found her where Totality indicated she would be. She is . . . different. Not like those in the 'hoods. This unit does not understand her."

Kim laughed lightly. "Nor does this unit, Erik. Whatever she is, though, I've got a feeling she may have saved Dunn's life. He hasn't rested this peacefully for two nights." She yawned. "Gods, I'm dead tired. I don't think I've slept more than a few moments for the last couple of days." She laid down and wiggled around to find a comfortable position. Once she was settled, she looked up to see the Ronin still sitting up, staring into the fire. "Erik, you've got to be dead on your feet. Why don't you go to sleep? If Dunn gets restless we'll hear him. Get some rest."

"This unit will rest later, Kim unit. Right now this unit wishes to think over recent events."

"What happened, Erik?" she asked softly.

There was such a long pause she thought maybe the Ronin had not heard her question. She was about to ask again when he finally spoke, his voice so quiet she almost missed it.

"This unit does not know. Does not know."

❧ Chapter 14 ❧

They came at her from every side, their blades swishing, their eyes glaring, animal screams bubbling from their drooling mouths. She knew there was no way to stand and fight so she turned and tried to run. Every step was agony. Her feet were so heavy and her legs just wouldn't move. Her robe kept getting between them and binding them. Hopelessly, she turned back to face her attackers. She reached for the sword at her side only to discover that it was gone, lost somewhere, sometime. Her attackers howled with glee and swarmed toward her. She wailed in utter, lonely fear.

And woke up to Erik's hand gently shaking her.

"Kim unit," the Ronin said, a slight frown creasing his forehead, "are you all right? You cried out. This unit—"

She held up a hand to reassure him and muttered sleepily, "Just an old dream. 's nothing." The Ronin sat back and watched her, clearly not satisfied with her answer. She closed her eyes for a second, then immediately opened them. Sleep had fled, and the darkness behind her own eyes bothered her. It was time to be up.

Turning, she looked over at the still form of Dunn. With a raised eyebrow, she queried Erik. He shrugged and said, "Dunn unit is resting better. He woke several times in the night with a high fever. The Kristina unit and this unit bathed his face to cool him down. But the fever has not broken. And the infection has not gotten any better. This unit still fears . . ." He let the words trail off as Kristina entered the shallow cave.

107

The woman in the black robe carried two handfuls of leaves and other plant parts. She nodded to Kim and spoke to the Ronin. "Here, these are some of the ones I was telling you about. Come, and I'll explain them and their properties to you."

Kim cleared her throat. "Ummm . . . Uh . . . how is Dunn doing?"

Kristina looked at her with a calm, open, and frank gaze. "Not well. The fever is still there. Very much so. The infection is bad, even worse than I thought at first inspection. But worst of all, we're going to have to move him."

"Move him?" both Kim and the Ronin said at the same time. "But he'll never survive a move," Kim continued. "I mean, he's too weak to walk and—"

"Not much choice," Kristina replied. "This cave is shallow and damp. There's a big storm coming. You can see the clouds piling up to the west if you go to the top of the ridge. Could rain for several days. That kind of cold and damp in his condition," she gestured to the prone figure of Dunn, "would just about end it for sure. Moving him is risky. Not moving him is worse."

She paused for a moment as if measuring their response. "Besides," she continued, "there's another, perhaps even more compelling reason. I came across Ronin spoor about a half hour north of here this morning. A camp. Maybe five or six of them." She let her gaze rest lightly on Erik. "I only see one sword here, other than Dunn's. That makes pretty poor odds against five, doesn't it?"

The Ronin looked down at the ground, then up to meet her gaze. "Yes," he said quietly and firmly. "One against five is very poor odds. Kim is probably good with her staff, but that helps only a little. This unit feels it would be best to find a more defensible or less easily found spot where Dunn has a better chance of recovering unmolested by rain or Ronin."

Kristina nodded. "A good decision. Don't you agree, Kim?"

The young woman nodded. "Five Ronin?" She cast a quick sideways glance at Erik. "Might be the group whose trail we crossed a couple of days ago. Where can we go, though?"

"We'll go to my cave. It's about three hours from here to the west. There's a sudden upthrust of rock there. It's pretty isolated and rather rugged, but the cave is large, has its own water supply, is dry and easily defensible." She paused and looked down at Dunn. "Three hours, that is, for a healthy man at a good pace. With him, it could take a hard eight. Best we get busy and make a stretcher of some kind to carry him. The sooner we leave the better. I don't like the looks of that sky, and I liked the looks of that camp even less."

Within an hour, they were on their way. Erik took the lead, holding the front end of the stretcher they had made from branches and vines. Kim and Kristina spelled each other on the rear end.

At first, their progress was fairly rapid. But the ground to the west rose quickly and became more and more broken. Dunn began to move about on the stretcher and occasionally a moan or soft cry escaped his lips. It was impossible not to bump and jostle him from time to time.

Kristina finally called a halt at the top of a ridge and said it was time to grab a quick bite to eat and to change Dunn's dressing. She also told the Ronin to go back over their path to see if anyone was following.

The two women worked over the restless body of Dunn. When the bandages were removed, Kim had to hold back her gorge. The sight and the smell of the wound almost made her sick. "It's . . . it's bad, isn't it?" she asked.

Kristina nodded as she worked. "Very bad. This bumping isn't helping any. Here, help me get this down his throat. It'll calm him a little, make the pain more bearable. Give him bad dreams, though." She sighed. "Can't be helped. Even the worst dreams can't be much worse than what he'd have to face if he was awake. He's strong, Kim. And determined. He's got a chance." She looked up at the dark, grim clouds, then back along the way they had come. "He's got a chance if we can only get him—"

Erik suddenly appeared, coming up the slope at a jog. He was frowning and his eyes were hard. He motioned the older woman to him. She handed Kim the bandage she

was wrapping Dunn's wounds with and went down to talk
with the Ronin. The two conversed in low tones, punctu-
ated with gestures aimed toward the north and east. The
conversation ended when Kristina said "No" in a very firm
manner and pointed toward Kim and Dunn.

For a moment longer, the Ronin hesitated, then nodded
and trotted up to the top of the ridge. He squatted next to
Kim and helped her finish her task. The young woman
tried to catch his eye, but the black-clad man purposely
kept his head down and his attention riveted to the
wrapping and securing of Dunn's wounds.

Kristina came and stood over them. When Kim looked
up at her with a questioning glance she simply nodded and
said, "Yes. The Ronin are out there. Erik came across
their tracks. We don't know if they've discovered our trail
yet. They might not. We must hurry." She looked up at
the threatening sky. "As much for that as for them."

As they started out once again, the wind began to pick
up. It was straight out of the west and felt heavy with cold
and rain. At times it came in sudden bursts which lashed
the trees and ripped leaves from them and hurled them
through the air.

The ground became more rocky and abrupt. Several
times they had to scramble down steep slopes, barely able
to keep their burden from tumbling into the deep ravines.
The climb up the opposite side was a grueling torture.
Kristina finally had them tie Dunn to the stretcher with
vine so he wouldn't roll off.

The wind blew a darkness before it, and it seemed as if
night was rapidly sweeping upon them. The clouds rolled
and twisted above them, reaching down with angry tenta-
cles as if to smash them from the ridgetops.

Their exhaustion grew with each step they trudged.
Even Erik's face was drawn and pinched with his effort.
While Kim and the older woman had taken turns at the
back end of the stretcher, he had carried the front end all
the way. And at every rest stop, he had gone back to
check their trail for sign of the Ronin.

The yipping howl was so close that Kim nearly dropped
the handles of the stretcher. All three of them stopped
dead in their tracks and listened. A second howl joined

the first from farther away. Then, from an even greater distance came a chorus of eager answering cries.

"Ronin," Kim said, her voice strangled and strange. Erik looked back at her and Kristina, his face twisted in an unreadable expression. "Five units," he said softly. The older woman nodded.

Kim sobbed a long shuddering breath of air into her lungs. Her whole body was shaking and her knees felt like water. She took a second breath and spoke rapidly. "Listen, both of you. Kristina, take my end of the stretcher. Erik, you keep yours. You're the strongest and the only way we'll get Dunn any farther is if you bear most of the effort. How far is the cave?"

"About another hour."

"Fine. Both of you get going. I'll follow more slowly until I find a good place to slow the Ronin down. That'll give you more time and—"

"No!" the Ronin said sharply. "No! You have no sword! They will kill you! There are five of them. You won't stand a chance. I will stay and delay them."

"Don't be a fool, Erik," Kim said sharply. "I can kill with this staff, but I don't intend to try and fight the whole lot of them. Just hold them off until the storm breaks, then escape in the rain. Damnit, Erik! We won't be able to get Dunn to the cave without you! Kristina and I aren't strong enough. You've got to go. Besides, once at the cave you could hold off a hundred Ronin with your sword. You're the only one who can guarantee safety for all of us! Now go, damnit! Before I change my mind!"

"Kim, no! I must fight. I must—"

"Damn you!" she shouted, tears coming to her eyes. "Damn you, go! Can't you . . . can't you see how frightened I am? Do you think I want to die? Get going before I'm too afraid to do it! Go! Go!"

Both Kim and the Ronin turned to Kristina as if to ask the older woman to settle the argument. She looked at them both, then nodded to Kim and took her place at the back end of the stretcher. "There is a narrow pass a short distance ahead. We must go through it. The ridge on either side is very steep and rocky. The only other ways through are several miles to the north or again to the southeast. It would make a good place to delay an army. It should serve quite well to delay five Ronin." Without another word she began to move forward, forcing the Ronin to move with her.

As soon as they were out of sight, Kim began to sob uncontrollably. Fear made her whole body feel weak and watery. It was impossible to even raise her hand. If she tried to move she knew her knees would give way and she would collapse in a heap. Then she began to shake so badly that her teeth chattered. A howl, followed by a chorus of other yelping screams snapped up her head and dried her tears instantly. The fear left her limbs and settled in a hard knot in her stomach.

The Ronin were close, she estimated. Probably not more than a mile off to the east. At the rate they could travel, even in this rough terrain, that meant they'd be upon her in about ten minutes. She turned and began to follow after the other three, hoping that the narrow pass would show up soon enough.

Fat, hard drops of rain, driven by the wind like tiny missiles, slammed into her face from time to time. Could she really escape in the confusion when the storm broke? she wondered. Would it break in time? Or would the wash of the rain simply clean the blood from her dead body? She shivered, but kept on moving.

At the top of one ridge, she heard a baying so loud and close, she turned and looked over her shoulder. There, on the opposite ridge, were five figures dressed in black. They saw her and raised a hideous howl, dancing about and waving their swords. Then they plunged down the opposite slope.

Trying to hold back her rising sense of panic, she began to trot. Where was that pass? If she didn't come to it soon, she'd have to fight them in the open. I'd last about two minutes, she estimated grimly.

She plowed through a dense growth of brush and saw a dark gap almost directly ahead in the side of a steep, rocky ridge. The ridge stretched off to both the right and left as far as she could see through the trees. The pass! Just in time!

Gasping for breath, as much from fear as from exertion,

she stumbled up the slight slope and into the slash of the narrow pass. Its rock walls were straight up and down, almost as if the opening had been cut in the ridge with a sword. An ominous rumble came from the sky and she looked up. The clouds were low and rushing by at an incredible rate. Fat bumps hung down from them, bulging toward her in a threatening manner. Off to the north a dull glow lit the sky for an instant. Another rumble sounded and another flash of light colored the rocks around her.

The Ronin burst from the trees at the base of the ridge and stopped, taking in the whole scene. Thunder crashed again and a bright flash of lightning ripped through the air so close by she could almost smell it.

Carefully, Kim backed into the mouth of the pass, making sure she was protected on both sides and the rear. She made a couple of practice swings with her staff to see if she had adequate room to maneuver. Satisfied with her battleground, she took her knife from its hidden sheath and stuck it in the back of the sash around her waist. Finally, she tucked her robe up in the front of the sash to keep it out of the way and stop it from catching on things as she moved.

The Ronin approached cautiously, unsure how many people held the pass against them. Unlike the killers of the past, the Ronin no longer attacked in mad, mindless fury. Now they fought almost as coolly and intelligently as ordinary men. They would assault en masse only if it seemed the best thing to do. Still they were fearsome fighters, unafraid of anything in combat. One would be a challenge for someone with only a staff. Five were impossible.

But, Kim reminded herself, they could only come at her one at a time through this narrow pass. At least, that's how the combat would begin. Perhaps after a few rebuffs they would rush her all at once. Then, she knew, no matter how hard she fought, she would be overwhelmed.

The Ronin were getting ready to try an attack to feel out the situation. Take your time, Kim silently told them. The longer you wait the farther Dunn, Erik, and Kristina will get.

A flash of lightning glared, momentarily blinding them all. Almost instantly, thunder crashed, its roar so loud it nearly knocked Kim to the ground. The sheer volume of the noise stunned the Ronin and halted them in midstride. Still, though, the rain did not fall. Even the wind had almost died out. Kim glanced up, half expecting to see the clouds standing still, but they roiled on eastward in ugly, dark masses.

With a cry, the Ronin charged the pass. One, a tall, dark-haired creature with straggly locks and mad, black eyes threw himself into the lead and was the first to spot Kim. Seeing one lone young woman armed only with a staff, he howled in victory and raised his sword on high to strike. Quickly, Kim stepped in and slammed the end of her staff against his right wrist. The blow was solid and powerful. The thwack of the wood against flesh was immediately followed by the crack of bone as the man's wrist broke. His sword stroke flew harmlessly to the right of Kim's shoulder. As he tried to recover his balance, the young woman reached behind her, grabbed her dagger and stepped in once more, the blade making a swish as it curved and sunk into his gut with a thud. The Ronin screamed once and then staggered back, one hand hanging useless, the other clutching his stomach. Blood flowed freely between his fingers.

The killer behind him tried to avoid the staggering man but was unsuccessful. They collided and the wounded man went sprawling while the second Ronin was thrown off balance. Kim took advantage of the situation, swiftly stepping in and jabbing the tottering man in the solar plexus with the tip of her staff. The blow doubled him over and she spun the staff around its own center, bringing the other end around in a hurtling arc to smash into the back of his bowed head. He went down like a rock.

Now the third one attacked, in balance and pre-warned that he was facing an opponent who was anything but a helpless girl. He jabbed at Kim's throat with incredible speed and nicked her shoulder as she half blocked his thrust with the tip of her staff. Then he stepped in, his sword swinging up for a head slash. Kim threw herself at him, her staff like a horizontal bar, and slammed into his body, the staff just above the man's elbows. For a second they tottered there, straining, locked in a contest of strength the man was bound to win. Suddenly Kim rammed her knee up into his crotch and he roared with pain. The young woman fell backward, stumbling, and nearly went down.

Her fourth opponent was on her in a flash. She was barely able to block his first blow. Stepping back from his second, she desperately tried to regain her balance and equilibrium. The man was pushing her back to a slightly wider part of the pass where two of them could attack her at the same time.

Kim fought with a fury she had never known she had. She blocked, parried, and attacked so strongly that the Ronin had to stop his advance and retreat. The fifth one took his place and she saw the one she had kneed getting up to rejoin the fight. Beyond him, the second man, the one she had knocked out, was beginning to come to.

Despair filled her heart. Even if she fought them one at a time, she would soon be worn out. They would wear her down and then it would be a simple matter to kill her. Exhaustion would slow her reflexes, weaken her blocks and attacks. Her wounded shoulder was already beginning to ache and stiffen. It was only a matter of time. A short time.

The wind hit her from behind with a rush and a blow that almost knocked her flat. It howled and tore at the pass and tried to rip the sky and earth to shreds. Thunder crashed and lightning slammed into the ground again and again as if the heavens were bombarding the earth. Dazed and stunned, she looked up in awe. The air was torn with flaring light. Branches and leaves flew like bits of straw. The very rocks beneath her shook in response to the fury of the storm.

Then the rain hit. Actually hit, like a fist or a club. It drove her to her knees and took her breath away. She tried to raise her head but could barely do it against the weight of the water sluicing from the sky. She couldn't see more than two feet in front of her.

Couldn't see! This was what she had been hoping for! The storm was here and she could escape. She turned quickly and staggered westward up the pass, bumping into rocks and the wall of the cleft as she went. Several times she stumbled and cut her hands against the rocks.

She reached the other side of the pass and realized she didn't have the slightest idea where to go. Doesn't matter, she told herself. Just head west. Put distance between yourself and the Ronin. No way they can follow in this storm. Couldn't track a Strider in this weather!

Kim laughed out loud. "I made it!" she exulted to the crashing thunder. "I'm alive! I held them off and gave the others time to escape!"

Thunder exploded directly over her head, beating her to her knees again. A slash of lightning lit the torrential downrush with an eerie, bluish glare, momentarily dazzling her eyes. In the afterglow she realized what she had seen and a whimper of fear rose in her throat.

A black-clad figure with burning eyes and a drawn sword had suddenly stepped out from behind the curtain of rain and was barring her way.

✪ Chapter 15 ✪

Her euphoria burst like a bubble, and Kim wearily fell back two steps into an onguard position, her staff held on her right side at a forty-five degree angle to the ground, its upper end squarely in front of her eyes. One of them must have circled me in the rain, she thought dully. Or else I got confused and went in a circle myself. She felt tears of hopelessness and frustration rise, but bit her lip hard to hold them back.

She waited for the killer to attack, staring hard at his body, trying to sense the moment he would launch himself at her. But something was wrong. The Ronin didn't attack.

Surprised and wondering, she let her eyes rise to the hooded face. And met the glowing blue eyes of Erik! The Ronin had a smile on his face. "Your reflexes are good, Kim unit, but you look tired and wet. This is the way to the cave. Come."

The young woman sagged to the ground in relief. "Oh, sweet shit, you scared the little bit of strength I had left right out of me, damn you!" she laughed wearily. "Gods! Help me up, Erik. I just killed a Ronin."

Erik stepped quickly to her side and pulled her gently to her feet. "Come," he repeated, "we must hurry. The Ronin are probably following. The trail to the cave cuts off here. If we go quickly the rain will hide our spoor and they will continue on west."

As swiftly as she could, the young woman followed the Ronin. The path was steep and unmarked, looking like any other piece of hillside. For several minutes they climbed, then went along a ridgetop, and finally descended a very steep incline along a trace that was barely wide enough for one person. Suddenly, there was an opening in the side of the cliff, about ten feet across and no more than seven feet high. They stepped through it, took about three steps, and found themselves inside Kristina's cave.

Kim gazed around in wonder. The cave was roughly rectangular, about thirty by twenty feet, with a twelve to fifteen foot ceiling. To the left of the entrance was a large cooking fire with two pots and a spit. Both pots were full and gently boiling. The aroma of food filled the air.

At the right rear of the cave was a low opening that Kim assumed led to another chamber. To the left of the opening she saw the sleeping figure of Dunn lying on a bed that appeared to be made of boughs. Here and there around the walls of the cave were simple shelves made from rocks and wood that held pots and bowls filled with everything from ko pods to strange roots and leaves.

But the most amazing feature of the cave were the walls. Kim gazed at them in open-mouthed wonder. Every available flat surface was covered either with tight, orderly lines of writing, or loose, fluid drawings.

She was about to walk over and get a closer look when Kristina came through the opening at the back of the cave. "Water's back here," she said by way of greeting. "Our own spring. Also another little chamber, about half the size of this one. A few even smaller ones beyond that. I use them for storage. Here," she held out a dry robe, "go back in there and change before you get any more chilled than you already are. And wash out that wound. It doesn't look deep, but you should keep it clean. I'll put something on it when you're done changing." Kim nodded and took the robe without speaking. She was simply too tired to think. As she stooped to enter the other chamber, Kristina said softly, "Congratulations. You made it. Thank you, from all of us."

When Kim came back, feeling tired but dry and deeply happy, Kristina and the Ronin were tending to Dunn's wounds. "You know," the older woman said over her shoulder to Kim, "I almost think that trip broke his fever! He seems a lot cooler now than before we left. Odd, that."

The younger woman went and knelt next to Dunn's head, laying her hand on his forehead. Kristina was right. The Earthman was definitely cooler. Perhaps the fever had broken. Oh, let it be so, she pleaded. Let it be so!

Erik went to the fire and came back with two bowls. One, filled with more hot water, he handed to Kristina. The other was filled with a dark, thick soup that smelled wonderful. He handed it to Kim. "Here, eat this, Kim unit. You have expended a great deal of energy today and need nourishment."

Kim laughed. "That, Erik unit, is putting it mildly! I could eat a whole Strider! Uncooked! In one bite!" With great relish, she took her eating sticks out of the pouch of the new robe and attacked the soup with great enjoyment.

When she had finished, Kristina came over and checked her shoulder wound. "As I thought," the older woman muttered beneath her breath, "clean, fairly shallow. Hmmmm. Nothing to get worried about." She rubbed a yellowish salve in the wound and bound the whole thing with a clean strip of cloth.

"Erik says you killed one."

"Yes," she nodded, "with my knife. At least I think I did. Stuck him in the stomach up to the hilt." She pulled back the hem of her robe and showed Kristina the knife strapped to her calf.

"Hmmmmmm. Yes. I think that might well kill a man. But if it was in the stomach he'll die slowly. Poor thing." She sighed sadly. "I guess it makes no sense to go looking for him. The others probably killed him. And anyway, its just too awful out there for travel right now."

"Not to mention that there are still four of his friends hanging around," Kim replied sarcastically. "You wouldn't really go out and help him, would you?"

"Why not?" the older woman shrugged.

"But," Kim protested, "he's a—" She stopped and shot a quick glance at Erik. "Oh, Gods, I'm sorry, Erik. I guess I . . ."

The Ronin waved away her apology. "This unit comprehends, Kim unit. This unit would not rescue a human in similar circumstances."

Kim turned back to the older woman. "But would you really rescue him?"

"If possible. One should treat all creatures equally. Compassion should temper every action."

"But . . . but . . . we're talking about Ronin!"

"We are all the same stuff. We come from the same source."

"Well," the younger woman said, unsure of Kristina's meaning, "yes, in a sense we did. I mean we all came on the Pilgrimage."

"I mean long before that, Kim. We are all merely aspects of the same unity, parts of a whole. Which spoke is it that holds the wheel? Can even one be removed without warping the circle and perhaps causing its ruin?"

"I . . . I don't understand."

"The Ronin, my dear, is of the same stuff as I am. We are all united in that which came before. It may not be pleasant to hear, but his value in the totality of things is equal to yours or mine."

Kim looked at the older woman, her curiosity aroused despite her bone-tiredness. "What do you mean by 'that which came before' and 'the totality of things'? I've heard about the totality of things before in the 'hoods. But I've got a feeling you mean something different by it."

Kristina smiled and put another piece of wood on the fire. "Yes, I mean something different from what you've heard in the 'hoods." Her voice took on a musing quality. "I entered a 'hood when I was young. Stayed for about eight years. Then I discovered I had not found the answers I was looking for." She laughed lightly. "I wasn't even asking the right questions! So I left. And Wandered. For ten years I walked up and down the eastern half of the Northern Continent, searching and searching. I saw good men die and bad ones live. I saw storm and fire fall on all alike. I saw the sun beat down and cause some shoots to flourish while others withered and dried up. I saw flowers bloom in glory only to pass into nothingness.

"My mother passed on. My father was lowered into the ground. A band of Ronin massacred my two brothers. My best friend was killed in a fall from a tree while picking ko pods for her children to eat.

"I Wandered and Wandered, looking for meaning. I searched within myself, the way I had been taught in the 'hood, seeking to dissolve the veil of seeming and pierce through to the ultimate reality of the point-instants.

"One day, many years ago, I ended up near here, weary and confused. In despair, I decided there was no hope. I made a resolution. One last time I would try to understand it all. I would sit beneath a ko tree and not move again until I had found what I wanted. If I died there . . . well, then I died."

The older woman laughed softly again. "Such a demanding person! I wanted the whole universe to stop what it was doing and answer my questions! Such ego!

"Well, I sat for two days. Then two more. The sun rose and set, rose and set. Lizards played around me, oblivious of my presence. A shoot began to grow between my legs, thrusting up out of the ground. It rained and the sun came out and dried the world. Two more days. Hunger was forgotten. It rained.

"I became delirious and faint. Visitors came and talked to me. My mother, father, brothers, everyone, even lizards had something to tell me. But none of them would answer my questions. None of them cared. The ko didn't care. The sprout, by then several inches tall, didn't care. The rain didn't care. The sun didn't care . . ."

She smiled in remembrance. "There I was, locked in my own body, angry and frustrated because no one and no thing gave a good damn about my questions. They seemed so real and so important to me and I had spent such a long time, and so much energy, to answer them. How could the universe not care?

"A little lizard crept up and invited me to see the world through his eyes. 'The trouble,' he said, 'is that you divide the universe into two parts, yourself and the rest. You go into yourself to learn about the part outside yourself. Your view of everything is subjective, and you make everything

else into objects. Try to go beyond the subjective. Put
yourself out and into the objects. See the world through
the eyes of the world.'

"I wept and told him I didn't understand. He turned
into a miniature ko tree that whispered to me with its
leaves. 'The Way has taught you to destroy the subjective
by going inside and annihilating the self by disintegrating
it into the point-instants, the disconnected, unrelated
here-nows of pure perception, and then letting it fall into
the void. They have told you to look closely at your
perceptions and sensations. See how fragmented, how
unrelated they are. Note well how they come and go in a
flash. These are the point-instants, the immediate here-
nows of Ultimate Reality. They rise and disappear without
pause. Nothing, they have told you, exists beyond them.
There is no solidity, no time, no space. These are all
illusions created by our imaginations. Concentrate, turn
inward, and they disappear. Even the self you are turning
inward to disintegrates into a billion impressions.'

"'This, they tell you in the 'hoods,' the ko rustled with its
leaves, 'is Ultimate Reality, the universe as it actually is.
And you must fall into the void between the point-
instants, the void that is even less than they are. There you
must find your wings and soar. You must believe.'

"The ko went away and an insect came in its place to
continue the teaching. Its voice was tiny but clear. It said,
'When you start your journey on the Way they tell you the
trees are just trees, the streams, streams and the mountains, mountains. But when you discover the reality of the
point-instants, when the everyday world breaks down into
the slippery nothingness of instant here-now, the trees are
no longer trees, the streams no longer streams, the
mountains no longer mountains. Then you must make the
leap of faith. You must reconstruct the universe, knowing
even as you do that it is an illusion you create. But now,
once more, the trees are trees, the streams, streams, the
mountains, mountains. Yet with a difference. For now you
have built them and can take them apart again at will. You
can put yourself in direct contact with them, return to the
direct perception of their point-instant nature. You have
transcended life and death by dismantling it. You have

soared over time and space by destroying it. Yes, that is what they teach you in the 'hoods.'"

She looked into the fire for long minutes. "Yes," she sighed, "if you turn inward and look in that way, that is precisely what you will find. The lizard, the ko, the tiny insect were right. I begged the insect to tell me more. 'What,' I asked it, 'should I do?'"

"Before the insect could answer, it was transformed into an ancient man, stooped and bent with age, but with a lively light in his eyes and a serene smile on his lips. 'What,' the old man said in a clear, bell-like voice, 'if you turn outward? What if rather than sinking into the obvious discontinuity of Ultimate Reality you let yourself soar into its equally obvious unity and coherency? What if you look at the forest rather than the tree? What if rather than destroying the self you transcend the self by projecting self into other, even let it become other? Destroy the two-fold universe! Annihilate the subjective-objective dichotomy! Flow outward to embrace the universe, beat with its rhythm, become one with it.'"

She paused and looked out of the cave toward the entrance where the rain still sluiced down in torrents. "All those years of being in the 'hood and Wandering, I had been searching for answers. Every day I had asked the same questions over and over in new ways. Every day I had tried to learn something new that would give me the answers I hungered for.

"The questions had grown and grown, but no solutions had ever come. I knew more, had seen more, experienced more, but still did not know what I wanted so badly to know. Why? How could such a thing be?"

She chuckled softly. "The lizard, the ko, the insect, the ancient had given me the answer. Rather than adding every day, I had to take away, to subtract day by day, hour by hour, those things that kept me apart from the universe.

"I had been asking the universe for answers, demanding them. In so doing, I was dividing things up into many, many parts. I saw good and bad, happy and sad, right and wrong, light and dark, narrow and wide, crooked and straight, ugly and beautiful. Dichotomies, opposites, conflicts. I railed against them and demanded that they be explained and justified.

"But who was I asking? Who or what was there to answer?

"My visions beneath the ko tree had told me. I was asking myself. As long as I stayed within myself, I could find no solutions because my subjective viewpoint, no matter how educated and experienced, was too narrow to encompass the whole universe.

"It opened to me then, like a door in the clouds that swings back to reveal the sunshine that lies beyond. Without leaving my hut I could know everything under the heavens. Without looking out my window I could understand the ways of the universe.

"For I am the universe. The universe is me. The answers lie within and without for I am within and without and the universe is within and without. We are not two. We are One.

"That was what I saw that day. And that is what I have been doing ever since. Rather than dissolving the universe, I have been trying to find its rhythm and flow and become one with it. Rather than running around the outside of the circle, I now stand in the center. I grasp the pivot where the *I* and the *not-I* meet and merge. I watch life follow death and death follow life. I see the possible become the impossible and the impossible become the possible. I view right turn to wrong and wrong to right. The flow of life around the circle goes on and on, altering circumstances and thus altering things themselves.

"And I see that in the end they are all the same thing. They are all reduced to the movement and flow of the Oneness that is the universe. No one thing takes precedence over another and all return whence they came.

"I stand at the pivot, the point where all affirmations and denials converge, the point from which all movements and countermovements join and become each other. There, the questions do not make much sense, because they are also the answers."

"I still don't have the answers to most of the questions I once asked. I've just stopped asking them. And in a way, I guess, they have been answered because they no longer plague me and drive me across the face of Kensho. Rather than a mystery, the world has become the place where I play and dance, myself with myself, myself with all, all with all.

"When the rain falls I no longer wonder why it falls on just and unjust alike. I spread my arms to it like a thirsty plant. When the sun is hot I no longer wonder why it destroys some while it nourishes others. I let it warm me and make me feel drowsy."

She stopped and looked at Kim and the Ronin with a slight smile. "Ah, but speaking of drowsy, you two are about to fall asleep sitting up!" She rose and went to the back of the cave. She returned with several blankets woven from the fibers of a plant that grew near streams. "Here," she said, "make yourselves comfortable. Don't worry about your friend Dunn. I'll watch over him."

"But aren't you tired?" Kim asked through a huge yawn she tried vainly to suppress.

Kristina chuckled. "I've spent so much of my life sleeping that I no longer need much. I'll watch."

Kim lay down. The fire was warm. The last thing she remembered was Kristina softly humming a tune that sounded a lot like the wind that came off the Plain.

⊘ Chapter 16 ⊘

Josh pushed himself back a little farther beneath the sagging roof of the 'steader's burned-out cabin. Damn, he thought, look at it rain! He gazed around at his shelter. Not much to brag about, he conceded. Just an abandoned shell with a corner and part of the roof still standing. But it was any port in a storm, and this was one devil of a storm! At least it would keep him dry. A drop of rain fell from above and he looked up to see water leaking through the roof overhead. Well, he sighed, at least mostly dry.

The storm had approached from the southwest, and the center of it appeared to be well south of him. What would it be like to be caught right in the middle of it? he wondered, wincing as the thunder roared and the lightning flared all around him.

He made himself as comfortable as he could, carefully estimating where the leaks would drop water and avoiding those spots as he took off his backpack and spread out his gear. Too wet for a fire, he decided, and took some cold vegetables and ken-cow cheese from his pack. No hot meal tonight, he grumbled. Ah, well, he thought philosophically, at least I'm not out in the forest someplace huddling beneath some tree and getting thoroughly soaked.

Finished with his meal, he carefully rewrapped the leftovers and put them back in his pack. Breakfast or lunch tomorrow, he thought. Can't afford to waste anything. The last 'stead he'd run across had been a good day north. The 'steaders had been generous and happy to see a

Brother in the area. They'd been nervous because one of them had come across traces of a group of Ronin not far to the south. Josh had found the tracks himself, but they had been several days old and appeared to be heading to the southeast.

The 'steaders had also told him there wasn't much in the way of people to the south of their place. A few families had moved down that way many years back. Several had been killed by one thing or another and those left had given up and returned. "Other side a the hills o'er there ta the east a bit ain't nuthin' but swamp and critters," one of the men had informed him. "Ain't e'en no Ronins. Nuthin' to kill what's worth the dyin'. Due south an a bit west ya'll run across a scattered 'stead or two, mostly right at the edge a the foothills."

Josh figured he had stumbled across one of the 'steader cabins that had been abandoned. He briefly wondered why. Had they just given up and headed back north again? Or had they been killed by Ronin? The cabin had been burned, but that didn't mean much, since 'steaders usually burned their cabins before they deserted a 'stead so that Ronin couldn't use it.

Would Ronin use an old 'steader cabin? he wondered idly. He looked out at the pouring rain and his mind drifted back over the last couple of days. He'd traveled slowly, taking a good deal of time to soak in the peace and quiet of the forest as he'd gone. Several times, when he'd found a particularly pleasing spot, he'd simply stayed for a while and let the beauty of it wash over his mind.

He hadn't realized how tired and tense he'd become. Every day he'd felt a little more of the tightness relax. Slowly, the knots in his mind were untwining and smoothing out.

Every now and then, his mind had drifted back to Myali, the Way-Farer, Judah, and all the others who were still struggling with the problem he'd wrestled with for the last five years. At those times, he'd feel a twinge of guilt. I should be there, working alongside them, he'd think. Then his sense of frustration would well up inside him.

He sighed now, thinking about it. No good. It had been

no good. He'd reached a total dead end and might as well admit it. That's why he'd decided to go Wandering. He'd failed and just couldn't face it. He'd run out.

Well, he admitted, maybe that was being a bit too harsh. He'd left, sure. But only because he had to establish a new way of looking at the problem.

So what had he accomplished so far? He shrugged. Not much. He had calmed down and cleaned out his mind a little. Now there was room for new ideas, at least.

For a few minutes, he sat mindlessly staring out at the rain, not thinking, not feeling, not doing much of anything. Then, without even a transition, he fell asleep.

It was still raining lightly when he woke up the next morning. He made a cold breakfast of the remnants of last night's meal and waited for the rain to stop. In a few hours it did. He packed up his things and stepped out into a sodden and dreary world.

For about an hour and a half, he walked more or less directly south. He was in a fairly wide and densely wooded valley. To the east he knew there was a range of sharp, rugged hills. Beyond that was a narrow strip of land that ended at the swamp. To the west was another range of hills, gentler, but higher, gradually rising into the foothills of the narrow mountain range that ran north and south parallel to the valley.

As the sun finally came out from behind the clouds to pay a brief visit, he came to an opening in the forest. In the center of it was one of the mysterious mounds that were spread up and down the east coast of the Northern Continent of Kensho.

He browsed around the base of the mound, looking for a smoothstone. None was to be seen. On a whim, he climbed to the top of the mound and looked around.

The view was much better than he had expected. For some reason, the trees in the area immediately around the clearing were all lower than the top of the mound. In addition, he noticed that in two directions he could see even greater distances. To the southeast he had a spectacular view. There was another to the northeast.

He gazed with pleasure to the northeast. Suddenly, he

noticed something in the far distance. He stared harder, trying to make sure, then swung to the southeast and stared again.

Excitement bubbled through his mind. Unless his eyes deceived him, what he saw in the far distance, both to the northeast and the southeast, were the tops of other mounds! How far off were they? As much as five miles or so. As far as he could see, in any case. They were very vague.

What could such a thing mean? Did it mean anything? Were all the mounds, all over Kensho connected in this strange way? Did the forest grow that way for a reason or was it only a fluke, one case in a million?

He found himself wondering about the mounds. What did anyone on Kensho know about them? Damn little, he realized. We assume they are the remnants of the civilization that brought the Mushin here and then were wiped out by the Mind Leeches.

Something suddenly struck him as odd, something that had never occurred to him before. If the mounds were the remnants of a prior civilization, why weren't there other remnants? So far as he knew, nothing like a ruined city or anything else had ever been discovered on either the Northern or Southern Continent. Of course, he admitted, the whole planet had not been carefully explored. But it was strange that *nothing,* not one trace, had ever been found. No, he admitted, it was more than strange, it was downright unlikely!

A civilization that had been capable of bridging dimensions would have had a pretty sophisticated technology. Probably immense sources of power. But there was no evidence of either on Kensho. No civilization, no cities, no ruins, nothing! He was positive that the original survey of the planet done by the flagship has shown no sign of power generation of any kind!

His mind was spinning. Why hadn't anyone ever thought of this before? he wondered. Perhaps it was just too obvious, and too unimportant for a race struggling for its very survival.

He sat down and turned the question this way and that, trying to see it from all sides. No matter how he looked at it, it came out the same: Their view of the mounds and the civilization that had made them was completely wrong and confused!

Work it out, he told himself, work it out. What if there had never been any civilization on Kensho? What if, his heart began to race, whoever had brought the Mushin to the planet had never lived here at all? *What if Kensho had simply been their laboratory, the site for an experiment too dangerous to conduct on a civilized world!?*

Damn! It made sense! Interdimensional research had to be dangerous. No creature in its right mind would conduct such an experiment in the middle of its own home. They'd keep it separate, away somewhere in case anything went wrong.

And something had gone wrong on Kensho. Horribly wrong.

Suddenly he could visualize the whole thing. The creatures, whoever and whatever they were, had come to the planet to conduct their experiment. They had succeeded in breaking through to another, higher dimension. But what had come raging through the hole had not been what they had expected. The Mushin had come, hungry, destructive. The Mind Leeches had undoubtedly annihilated the creatures, just as they had attacked the doomed members of the Pilgrimage. They had left no civilization behind because they had brought none. It was someplace else, on another planet.

Where? came the immediate question. Someplace within the same system as Kensho? No, that couldn't be. The flagship had made a thorough search of the whole system, every rock, to be sure there was no dangerous life before pilgrims had been set down on the surface. It had to be somewhere else. Somewhere in the vast reaches of space.

Neither he nor anyone else had any way of finding out.

Would they come back? Not likely. If anyone had survived the massacre, they would have spread the warning. If no one had survived, well, that spread the warning to the home planet just as effectively. No, the odds were against them ever coming back. And if they ever had, it would have been a long, long time ago.

But what did that tell about the mounds? Clearly they

were not the remnants of a civilization, but rather the remnants of an experiment. They were the broken and abandoned alembics and crucibles of an ancient alchemist's lab, covered with the dust and neglect of years. And the smoothstones? More of the same.

Had the mounds and smoothstones played an important part in the experiment? he wondered.

Then a new thought crossed his mind. Were the mounds and smoothstones *still* playing a part in the experiment? The fact that the forest grew in a particular way near the mounds seemed to indicate that the mounds were capable of exerting an influence around and between themselves. An influence that was still effective how many years after the experiment? A thousand? Two thousand? A million?

He looked nervously around as if expecting to see some sort of glowing radiation coming from the mound. There was nothing. There never had been. At least nothing that he or any other human had ever been able to see or detect.

But then, he thought uneasily, we weren't able to detect the Mushin, either. Not even with all the resources of the flagship.

What *were* the mounds? Were they some kind of machine? Some kind of energy source? Or were they simply big humps of dirt?

His mind took off on another tack. If the mounds had had something to do with the experiment, that meant they had something to do with the Mushin. And, so had the smoothstones.

He took his out of the pouch on the front of his robe and looked at it. A smooth, featureless, roughly ovoid shape with an unremarkable, dull white finish. It appeared to be nothing but a stone worn smooth by the waves of the ocean. Yet it was not a mere rock. Whatever it was made of was virtually indestructible. Even a diamond wasn't sharp enough to scratch its surface. Furthermore, it was always about the same temperature, just slightly cool to the hand. And smooth, so smooth, he thought as he ran his thumb absently over the surface. Why did every Kenshite want one? he wondered. Everyone went out looking for them. A few lucky ones found them, always at the base of the mounds.

Were the mounds and the smoothstones somehow tied together in a way that went beyond mere proximity? A wild thought crossed his mind. Did the mounds *produce* the smoothstones? Was that why they were only found around their bases?

His mind hurt from all the questions. There were so many! So many that no one had ever asked. He briefly wondered if he should call Myali or some of the others to tell them what he had discovered.

But then, exactly what had he discovered? And why should anyone else be interested in it? Why, for that matter, was he so interested?

Because, he told himself, it had something to do with the Mushin, and anything that had to do with the Mushin was of interest. He was still convinced the answer to the problems Kensho faced lay, somehow, in the Mind Leeches. There was no way to justify his feeling. He just knew it was true.

This, he decided, was one he'd have to tackle on his own. He felt excited. He had something to do, something to put his mind to.

How, though, to go about it? He thought for several moments and could come up with no scheme for attacking the problem. It was unique. There was virtually nothing to go on but his own speculations and suspicions. The problem had no form because it had no starting point and no ending point.

He shrugged. There was only one thing to do. Jump in with both feet and see where it took him. Open up his mind to even the wildest speculations and ideas. Count nothing as too absurd until it was proven wrong. This was a problem he'd have to attack at odd angles, trying to catch it unaware.

What next? He stood and looked around. The view to the southeast caught his eye. Should he see if he could follow the forest to the next mound? Why not? He knew what to look for—slightly shorter trees. If he couldn't detect any differences from the forest floor, he knew the direction of the next mound and could simply hunt around until he found it.

He wondered what he'd see from that mound. Only this

one? Or would the forest around it behave in exactly the
same manner and give him a view of other mounds?
Worth finding out, he decided.

Settling his pack on his back, he set off down the mound
and into the forest, heading southeast. He was happy for
the first time in several years.

His high spirits lasted about half an hour. That was
when he came across the tracks of a party of four or five
Ronin. The trace was recent, made since the storm. The
group was heading in the same direction as he was.

Should he turn aside? He debated with himself. He
didn't like the idea of following a bunch of Ronin. It would
be too easy for them to ambush him if they realized he was
behind them. Yet if he turned aside, would he be able to
regain his bearings and find the mound?

For several moments he stood indecisively. Then his
burning curiosity about the mounds and their connection
with the Mushin got the best of his sense of caution and he
began to head once more in the southeasterly direction,
dead on the path left by the Ronin.

With a grim smile, he loosened the cords that held his
sword in its scabbard, keeping his right hand lightly on the
hilt of the weapon. If they do try to ambush me, he
thought, they'll find no easy prey.

❧ Chapter 17 ❧

Josh looked over the Keeper's shoulder. "Does it make any sense to you?" he asked. "I started drawing it after I realized how complex it was."

The old woman looked up at him. "Why don't you sit down and relax? This might take a while. There's something familiar about it, but I can't quite place it. How did you get it again?"

Josh sighed as he sat across the table from the Keeper. "Took me six months of tramping all over this part of Kensho." He pointed at the diagram that lay on the table between them. "Those dots represent mounds. The lines are the lines that connect them. Usually you can see them because the trees are shorter in that direction. In open areas, though, it's harder."

He pulled himself closer to the table. "See there? That's the coastline. Somewhere off the coast there must be more of them under the sea. Otherwise there would be breaks in the pattern, lines that lead nowhere, that kind of thing. That doesn't seem right. I'm sure they're there.

"All in all, I visited 26 mounds. Every mound had six lines leading away from it. I didn't realize that at first. Some of the lines are clearer than others, so I missed a few at the beginning."

Josh sat back and gave the Keeper a meditative look. "I took this drawing to several other Keepers. None of them could make heads or tails of it. But Keeper Marvin suggested you might be able to figure it out. I'm sure it means something. The whole system of mounds and lines had to be built by whoever brought the Mushin here. I'm sure it has significance, but I'm afraid it's beyond me."

The old woman waved him to silence as she began to concentrate on the drawing. Her brow furrowed and she muttered under her breath. "No, no, not that. Hmmmm. But perhaps? No, makes no sense." For many minutes she went on, turning the drawing this way and that, frowning anew and continually muttering to herself.

Finally, she looked up, a gleam in her eye. "Problem is," she began, "we're only looking at part of the whole pattern. That's the problem. It's the *six* lines radiating out from each point that are confusing the issue. Aren't enough points to account for all the lines."

Josh blinked at her in confusion. "Do you know what it means?"

She shook her head. "No, I don't know what it means. But I do understand what it is. The trick is simplifying it so it's easier to see. Hmmm. Look, let's take just this area here." She pointed to one part of the diagram.

Josh looked at where she pointed, then up at her. His expression was one of utter befuddlement. "Sorry. All I see are a bunch of points and lines."

"Hmmm. Let's simplify then." She took a piece of paper out of a drawer in the table and began to draw on it with a thin brush dipped in ink. "First an octagon. Then on the inside of each face of the octagon, a square. So." She held it up for Josh to see. "Still doesn't mean anything, does it? See, it's the same as this part right here in the diagram you made up."

Josh nodded. "I can see that, but I still don't—"

She held up her hand to stop him. "Wait. I'm not done simplifying. Let's draw a square here, another one, slightly overlapping, here, and join their vertices with four lines."

"That I can see. That's a cube."

She smiled. "No, it's just a two-dimensional representation of a cube. We recognize its three dimensionality by a visual convention. Can you see it in the first drawing I made? It's right there. And there. Several places. The first drawing is similar to the second in that it too is a two dimensional representation of a higher dimensional object. But in its case, the object it represents is a four-dimensional figure called a hypercube."

"Hypercube? I've never heard of it. What . . . ?"

The old woman smiled again. "The best way to explain a hypercube is start at the beginning with the simplest figure of all." She marked a single dot on the paper. "A point has no dimensions. Except time, of course, but that won't count in this discussion. Now," she touched the brush to the dot and extended it into a line. "When you move a point in a direction not contained within itself, it becomes a line, a one-dimensional figure. Move the line," she drew a square, "in a direction not contained in itself and it becomes a two-dimensional plane, a square, in this case." She looked up to see if Josh was following her. "If I move the plane in a direction not contained within itself, what do I get?"

"A cube!" Josh responded.

"Well, I will if the plane is a square. What I get is a three-dimensional figure. Now suppose I move the cube in a direction not contained within itself?"

Josh frowned. "I . . . I can't imagine that. A direction not contained in itself?"

"Yes. Or if it makes it easier to visualize, a direction ninety degrees from any other."

"But . . . but . . . there aren't any!" Josh protested.

"Right," the speaker nodded. "There aren't any. At least not any that can be understood in three-space. In the same way that a being in two-space couldn't understand the idea of something moving at a ninety degree angle to the two directions it comprehends, neither can a being in three-space easily understand a direction ninety degrees from the three it knows. It doesn't make common sense.

"Now, remember what I said about our drawing of the cube? It was a two-dimensional representation of a three-dimensional figure. Notice how it's made. Two of the axes, call them X and Y, are at right angles to each other, so. The third, Z is forty-five degrees to the other two. That's strictly a convention, but it helps visualization. And if a two-dimensional theoretician could postulate the idea of a three-dimensional cube, he could represent it in just such a fashion, even if he couldn't see it the way you and I do.

"Now look at the first figure I drew again. What do you notice?"

A look of wondering comprehension began to dawn in Josh's eyes. "Its made up of several cubes if you look at it right. And . . . and . . . yes," he said, beginning to be excited with his discovery, "the new lines are at forty-five degrees from two of the other lines!"

"Very good. What does that suggest to you?"

The look of wonder was complete now. "This . . . this is a two-dimensional representation of a four dimensional object!"

The old woman laughed. "Dead right! As I said earlier, it's a hypercube, a cube moved in a direction not contained within itself, that direction being toward the fourth dimension."

Josh sat and pondered the series of drawings the Keeper had made. He finally looked up and frowned. "But my drawing is much more complex than a hypercube."

"True," she nodded. "Your drawing is part of a hyper-hyperhypercube. That is, a cube in six-dimensional space. The cube was undoubtedly chosen because it is one of the three regular polytopes possible in N-dimensional space when N is greater than five. The other two are the tetrahedron and the octahedron."

"Are you saying that the mounds are a two-dimensional model of a six-dimensional space?"

"Something like that. A hypercube has sixteen vertices with four lines leaving each vertex to make up thirty-two edges, twenty-four plane faces. A hyperhypercube has thirty-two vertices with five lines leaving each vertex to make up eighty edges that bound eighty plane faces. You only mapped twenty-six vertices, but each one had six lines leaving it. That could only be a hyperhyperhypercube."

"But what in Jerome's name could it mean?"

She shrugged. "I said I knew what it was, not what it meant."

Josh sat and stared off into the corners of the cell for

several moments. Then he shifted his gaze back to the old woman. "We've always believed," he began hesitantly, "that the Mushin came from another dimension." The Keeper nodded. "We've believed that all we see is the part of them that 'sticks' into our space. Could they be from six-dimensional space?"

"It's possible," she began slowly. "Of course, they wouldn't have to be from that high a space. Snatching, for example, could be accomplished by beings from four-space."

Josh looked interested. "How? I've never quite understood how Snatching works."

"Hmmm. Well, the best thing is to simplify again. Let's look at two-space, a plane. The interior of a square drawn in two-space would be invisible and impenetrable to any creature in that planar two-space. Put a hinge at one corner and it would make a good safe, or if it was big enough, a house.

"To a three-spacer, however, the square is wide open at the top, that is, in the direction of the third dimension. Such a creature could reach right into the square, take out whatever was there, and make off with it. The two-spacers would be mystified, unable to understand how the object in the square disappeared.

"Now take that to three-space. Imagine a room with no windows or doors, one totally closed to three-spacers. To a four-spacer, the room would be wide open in the direction of the fourth dimension. The four-spacer could reach right in and take anything from the room without disturbing the walls.

"That's what the Mushin do, Josh. They simply move us in the direction of a higher dimension and then set us back down again. No reason why they have to be anything more than four-spacers to do that. Equally, no reason why they couldn't be six-spacers."

"Why can't we move ourselves into four-space?"

The old woman laughed. "Nothing to push against! We can move in three dimensions because we can exert a force in the direction of those dimensions. But we can't exert one in the direction of the fourth dimension because it doesn't exist in three-space!

"Oh, I guess in a way we can. You see, three-space is curved in the direction of the fourth dimension, just the way the two-dimensional surface of a sphere is curved in the direction of the third dimension. Creatures on the two-dimensional face of the sphere wouldn't *see* the curve, although there are ways to measure it if you have long enough rulers and enough time." She chuckled. "Let's not get into that, though."

Josh frowned. "I thought our space was curved by gravity."

"That's one way of looking at it. Mass distorts space in its vicinity, curves it if you will. Objects moving near the mass seem to be attracted to it. The paths they follow are geodesic lines that define the curvature of space in that area. The total mass of the universe likewise causes all of space to curve. That curvature defines the geodesics, that is, the 'shortest' lines in space, just the way the curvature of the sphere will define the geodesics of its surface, that is, what we call 'great circles.'

"But the creatures on the surface of the sphere might just as easily say that the geodesics are caused by a mysterious force that causes all the shortest lines to follow a certain curvature. There might be variations here and there because of roughness on the surface, but overall, the force exerts a universal influence over any object moving on the surface of the sphere, forcing it to follow the great circle path if it wishes to follow the shortest path. Thus a bullet would always follow a great circle path.

"Now, we say our space is curved by gravity. Curved in what direction? Obviously, the fourth dimension, just the way the two-dimensional surface of the sphere is curved toward the third dimension. And just as surely as in the case of the sphere, the curvature may be caused by the fourth dimension instead of by a posited universal force, that is, gravity. So it is the curvature in the direction of the fourth dimension that causes objects in our universe to move as they do, along their geodesics. In a sense, any moving object in our three-dimensional space is moving in the direction of the fourth dimension, even if not in the fourth dimension itself."

Josh thought for a moment, then shrugged. "I guess I

sort of understand what you're saying. I just wish I could understand what the pattern of the mounds means. It's got to have significance and I'm convinced it has something to do with the Mushin."

It was the Keeper's turn to give a questioning glance. "Something to do with the Mushin? What do you mean?"

"I have this idea," Josh began hesitantly. "Could be just so much nonsense, but somehow I don't think so. You know, we've never found any trace of the civilization that brought the Mushin here. Nothing but the mounds. So I wonder if the mounds are really some kind of apparatus used in the interdimensional research of that civilization. Maybe Kensho is nothing but a laboratory planet, a place to safely conduct dangerous experiments. Maybe they never lived here." He shrugged. "A lot of maybes. But there's something there. Something."

The Keeper was looking down at Josh's drawing, frowning in concentration once more. "Maybe," she said slowly, "maybe the mounds aren't so much an apparatus as a habitat."

"A what?" Josh asked.

"A habitat. A re-creation, in simplified terms, of the six-dimensional space the Mushin inhabit. You know, the way a biologist sets up a cage when he wants to study an animal in captivity. Maybe the mounds form a sort of habitat for the Mushin to live in so they can be studied in as near to their own environment as is possible in three-space."

For several moments Josh just stared at the woman, the light of discovery slowly growing in his eyes. "By the Gods, you could be right! Or what if the mounds are something even more than a habitat? What if they're a trap, a way to lure a six-dimensional creature to a certain area of three-space so it can be studied?"

The Keeper nodded. "Why not both? A trap and a habitat. Lure the creature and then cage it in a place similar to its own home. We do almost the same thing to animals we wish to study."

Josh shook his head in amazement. "Yes! It all fits! They build a trap on a laboratory planet and bait it with the pattern of the mounds to mimic six-space. The Mushin

come, they slam the door shut and the beast goes wild.
They couldn't have known too much about the Mushin.
They were taking a terrible chance. And the whole thing
backfired! The beast in the cage wiped out its captors!
Then the beast couldn't get out again. It was stuck,
trapped and slowly dying until we came along. Gods!
Incredible! But it just might be true."

He began to pace back and forth in the Keeper's cell.
"That could explain the purpose of the mounds, but a big
piece of the puzzle is still missing."

"What's that?" the Keeper asked.

"The mound pattern may have brought the Mushin
here. But what keeps them here? How do you close a
three-dimensional cage on a six-dimensional creature?
You said earlier that a three-dimensional person could
reach right inside a two-dimensional safe and take out its
contents by moving them in the direction of the third
dimension. What is stopping the Mushin from simply
moving out of the cage in the direction of a higher
dimension?"

"Perhaps," the Keeper mused, "the cage has six-
dimensional walls."

Josh stopped his pacing and stared at her.

✦ Chapter 18 ✦

Dunn sat in the narrow entrance of the cave and gazed out at the fine drizzle of rain. He could just see the tops of the trees in the narrow valley below the cave. They were shiny with moisture, their bluish-green color intensified. There was virtually no wind, yet the leaves moved constantly as drops of rain hit them. The millions of tiny collisions filled the air with a soft murmuring.

He liked to watch the rain fall. It soothed his mind and made him pleasantly drowsy. Almost nothing seemed to matter when the sky clouded over and a steady rain slowly soaked the earth. Everything seemed to be held in abeyance, waiting, waiting.

Storms, of course, were vastly different. Then the air howled and the trees shivered in fear as the rain slashed down, ripping the very earth apart in its anger. There was no peace, no soothing calm in a storm.

He wondered idly where Kim and Erik were and what they were doing. Was the rain falling on them, too? Probably. Kristina never sent them very far in their searches. Only to mounds fairly close by.

Why was Kristina so interested in smoothstones anyway? She'd taken his and Kim's. What did she do with them? The three that the Ronin and the young woman had found recently had disappeared into the pocket of the older woman's robe after a close scrutiny, and had never been seen again. She must keep them somewhere, though he knew it wasn't here in the main cave, nor in either of the two smaller chambers behind it. After six months, he would have noticed them if she had.

Six months. He moved his left leg. It always ached slightly when it rained. He pulled up the hem of his robe and looked at it. The calf was a mass of twisted white scar tissue where the swamp creature had torn it and where Kristina had had to cut away the rotten flesh. He still limped when he walked. Kristina said he always would. Only one hand and one leg, he thought.

He laughed softly. One hand, one leg! He'd better be careful! This planet kept whittling away at him. What would go next? What was there left to go? He smiled. By Kuvaz, it was damn good to be alive, sitting here watching the rain, his leg gently aching. Damn! He'd been so close to death. First the creature. Then the infection. Nothing like a little dying to make you appreciate living!

His mind turned to the mystery of the smoothstones again. Kristina had sent Kim and Erik out three times now to search for them. Why did the woman want them? What did she do with them?

He stood slowly, pulling himself up with the crutch Kim had made for him. Awkward, he thought, but getting better every day. He knew that Kristina had left the cave early this morning to gather herbs and food in the forest. And, he suspected, to visit a nearby mound that had still failed to yield a smoothstone. This was a good opportunity to give the cave a thorough going over.

For a second, he felt a little twinge of guilt at the idea of searching Kristina's cave. If not for her, he would have died. In all truth, he had no right to pry into the woman's affairs, strange or not. But curiosity quickly overcame his guilt, and he began to hobble about.

The main cave didn't hold much. There was the cooking fire, situated so that the smoke from it could exit easily through the mouth of the cave. His sleeping place was there by the left wall, right near Erik's. Kim slept in the small chamber that opened off to one side, and Kristina occupied the remaining one. He had never really been in it.

The most amazing thing about the main cave was the drawings and writing that covered the walls and part of the ceiling. Some were poems, a few koans, but the vast majority seemed to be formulas of some esoteric type.

They made no sense whatsoever to him since he didn't recognize any of the symbols. He'd asked Kristina about them once, but she'd just smiled and said they were her way of thinking things out. When he'd asked what kind of things she was thinking out, she'd changed the subject.

The drawings were equally bizarre. Some were clearly very fine copies of flowers, plants, herbs, insects, and lizards that could be found in the area. Several were strange landscapes that disoriented his eye, the perspectives twisted and disturbing. The rest looked like geometric patterns, lines and points joined together in odd profusion. In a way, they reminded him of circuit drawings, but not of any circuits he had ever even imagined.

There was nothing hidden anywhere here, he decided, and hobbled, stooping, through the low entrance into the second chamber. This was Kim's room and a storeroom as well. Here Kristina kept dried herbs and foodstuffs like ko pods. He moved slowly around the small room, searching carefully, touching nothing. After about ten minutes he admitted the search was a failure. There were no smoothstones here.

The Earthman had to stoop even lower to enter Kristina's room. Once inside he stood and looked around. On the wall to his left was a magnificent drawing, an abstract filled with color and shape. He stared at it in fascination, drawn into it against his will. For several minutes his eyes moved around the drawing, pulled and pushed this way and that by the lines and shapes and hues that tumbled in an alien order across the face of the rock wall. Finally, he came to a gap, an ending, a vast chasm where understanding stopped dead and the drawing abruptly ended. He shook his head to clear it, his eyes still dazzled and confused. This must be new, he thought vaguely. I'm sure it wasn't here the last time I looked into this chamber.

Turning away from the drawing, he scrutinized the rest of the room. It was spare and simple. A pallet to sleep on. A crude chest to hold clothes. A low table and a cushion. The top of the table held several brushes and three bowls filled with dried pigments.

As he moved to the table, his eye was caught by an

irregularity in the opposite wall of the cave. The torches had been placed very carefully, he realized, to make the wall look as smooth as possible. He limped over to the wall and discovered a narrow slit about two and a half feet wide and perhaps five feet tall. It was hidden behind a slight projection in the wall and could only be seen from the side.

Cautiously, he peered into the opening. It was so dark he couldn't see anything, but he had the feeling of a large empty space. He wet his finger and held it up. Yes. There was a very slight flow of air coming out of the opening.

Taking the nearest torch, he began to squeeze himself carefully through the opening. He moved slowly, checking the floor in front of him to be sure the footing was good. There wasn't enough room here for his crutch.

The passage he was following was fairly short. After a few steps, it widened abruptly. Dunn's torch simply didn't cast enough light to reach to the limits of the space he entered. He felt dwarfed and awed by the immensity of the cavern. He and his torch were a mere spark in a vast blackness. Involuntarily, he shivered.

His eyes lowered to the floor of the cave and his breath came in a gasp of surprise. Smoothstones! For several moments, he simply gazed in wonder and tried to take it all in. The smoothstones were laid out in a pattern, joined with lines of many hues. Here and there, the smooth-stones were surrounded with an aura of color carefully painted around them on the floor of the cave. The overall effect was startling and vaguely familiar. He stared and stared and suddenly realized that the whole intricate pattern reminded him of the drawing on the wall in Kristina's chamber!

Carefully, keeping away from the lines and colored areas, he walked around the pattern. Yes! There was the gap, the hole, just like in the drawing! And this part was like that mad swirl of energy and color in the upper righthand corner! As he wondered he began to realize there was a second level of connections between the smoothstones. If he allowed his eyes to go slightly out of focus, some of the smoothstones seemed to recede while others came forward. He knelt down and looked at the lines. Some of them were thicker than others, some seemed to taper forward or back. He stood again and unfocused his eyes. Yes! The pattern gave the illusion of being three dimensional!

He continued to stare at the strange pattern until his head began to ache and his eyes blurred with tears. The more he looked the more bizarre and unsettling the whole thing seemed. It had a sense of movement and energy, an ability to shift perspectives that disturbed him and made him slight queasy.

What in the name of Kuvaz is the damn thing? he wondered. It made no sense. No, that wasn't true. It did make a strange kind of sense, but not one he could wrap his mind around. Alien, that's what it was. Alien.

Could the smoothstones be somehow alien? He had carried one for years and had never felt any sense of the alien from the thing before. On the contrary, there was something oddly soothing about holding a smoothstone and gently rubbing it with the thumb or fingers.

But he'd never been near so many of them at the same time. Nor had he ever seen them laid out in a pattern like this. He looked at the pattern again. There was a sense of rightness about it, a sense of energy flowing correctly even if strangely.

Abruptly, he decided he had to see the drawing on the wall in the other room again. He turned from the smoothstones with one last look and left the vast, dark chamber.

In front of the drawing once more, he allowed it to draw him in completely this time. He gave up his own will and tried to surrender utterly to the logic of the drawing. After numerous attempts, he realized it was hopeless. Up to a point he could do it, then the drawing would take some totally incomprehensible twist that left him floundering and lost. It seemed grander and fuller than the smoothstone pattern in the other room and yet it lacked the energy and sense of power the pattern had given him.

For a moment, he wondered whether that sense of power had been a result of the pattern alone, or if the smoothstones had somehow actually been sending off emanations of energy. It almost sounded too foolish to consider, but after the experience of seeing and feeling both the pattern and the drawing, he decided nothing was unlikely.

A new idea struck him, and he limped his way back to the main chamber again. Carefully, thoughtfully, he looked at the drawings there that he had never been able to understand before. It took a long time, but he finally felt sure he had identified at least two of them that resembled either parts of the larger drawing or of the pattern. Were they studies for the more complete works?

His leg was hurting with a dull, throbbing ache. Too much standing, he realized in surprise. I've been on my feet for several hours! He limped back to the cave entrance. The rain had stopped and it looked like the sky was opening up to the west. He sat down.

What did it all mean? The drawings in the main cavern, the larger one in Kristina's chamber, the pattern of smoothstones in the hidden cavern. Clearly they were all related. Just as clearly, they all had some sort of meaning. Was it human meaning? He almost thought not. It seemed so alien to him.

And what did that say about Kristina? Obviously, she was responsible for all of it. She was the one who had made the drawings, collected the smoothstones, laid them out in the pattern. She must, therefore, understand the pattern. Did that mean that she wasn't human? Or that at least her mind wasn't?

What could the purpose of it all be? Why collect smoothstones in the first place? Why put them in patterns? Why make drawings that somehow reflected those patterns? His head spun with all the questions until it ached as much as his leg.

What should he do about his discovery? Kristina had never told them why she had wanted the smoothstones. They had simply followed her orders without questioning her. On the other hand, he had to admit she hadn't really hidden anything from them. The cave had been there the whole time. None of them had ever inquired.

Would the woman answer his questions if he asked? Probably. She always did. Should he show Kim and Erik what he had found? Or should he just keep quiet and wait and see what developed?

He heard a sound from outside the cave. He stretched out and peered around the edge of the opening. There on the narrow path that led to the cave's mouth, he saw two figures carefully approaching. Kim and Erik were returning. Kristina would doubtless be back fairly soon as well.

He would have to decide pretty quickly what to do.

❧ Chapter 19 ❧

The four of them stood in the flickering light of the torches and gazed at the pattern on the floor of the cavern. Even now, with four torches, Dunn could still not make out the walls or ceiling of the vast empty space. It made him shiver slightly to think of the size of the empty darkness around their small island of light.

Kristina had just placed the smoothstone Kim and Erik had returned in its place amongst the others. "Yes," she said, rubbing her hands together delightedly as she stood. "Yes, it fits right where I thought it would. An outer boundary apex. Now if only I could find that one," she pointed to a place in the pattern, "then we would have a complete substructure of the fourth order." She looked up and smiled at them. "Those terms are my own. I made them up because there didn't seem to be any in ordinary language that matched."

Kim looked at her with awe. "How . . . how did you do all this?"

"How? Hmmmmm. That's not as important as why, but I'll try to answer both at the same time. Once, oh, long ago, I was trying to find an object to focus my meditation on. That's an old trick, but at the time I needed anything to help. The object should be something relatively simple to help the mind concentrate. By sheer chance, I had found my second smoothstone the day before, so I decided to use it as a focus.

"Something strange happened as I began to concentrate on it. I seemed to sense a sort of energy coming out of it. I could almost imagine an aura of force surrounding it.

149

Once I had imagined it, I could actually see it. In surprise, I took out my other smoothstone and tried the same thing with it. The results were identical, except that the auras were quite different.

"The whole thing intrigued me a great deal and I spent several weeks working with the two smoothstones, separately and then together. Together, they created a new field of force through some kind of interaction.

"At the time, it all seemed nothing more than a fascinating, but useless, piece of information. Then I found a third smoothstone. And a fourth. All had that sense of energy and each one was distinct and yet somehow integrated with the other three. Not closely, mind you, but in some way I couldn't understand.

"I still don't understand, but I begin to see that the pattern is far greater, far more complex than I thought." She looked at the three of them. "Can any of you feel their power?"

Kim spoke first. "Looking at the pattern, I can feel . . . something. But it's hard for me to look at it for very long. I can't quite find the words to express how it makes me feel. The pattern seems right . . . yet it's wrong somehow."

The Earthman nodded. "Yes. It's wrong. Not in the sense that there's a fault in the pattern. I guess I felt it was wrong in the sense of being somehow not *here*. It seems alien to me."

Kristina nodded. "It *is* alien, Dunn. I'm convinced the smoothstones are the handiwork of the race that brought the Mushin to Kensho. I don't know what they are or what they do, but I've worked with them for many years now. This pattern is right. I don't know why, but I just feel it is. The energy seems to flow correctly."

Kim shivered involuntarily. "I don't like it. It seems to go on and on, to some place else, some place humans don't belong. Erik, what do you think?"

For the first time, the three of them looked at the Ronin. Erik stood there, rigid, his face blank, his eyes empty, a fine sheen of sweat on his forehead and upper lip. He looked like a man in the grip of a strange dream. "Erik!" Kim shouted in alarm.

The young woman's cry brought life back into the black-clad man's eyes. Slowly his face relaxed and he slumped slightly. "This . . . this unit was with Totality. Totality does not like this place. No. It is not that Totality does not like it. It is very comfortable. It is that it holds Totality too tightly."

Kristina's eyes shone with interest. "What do you mean? How does it hold Totality?"

"This unit lacks words to explain. This unit cannot really comprehend the meaning of Totality. Somehow . . . somehow this pattern restricts Totality. It is not unpleasant. It is burdensome. It . . . it forces Totality to concentrate. No, that is not quite right. This unit cannot understand! This seems to be a transfer point, a place of staying before passing on, a junction between two somethings, neither of which exist here-now but which include here-now. It is . . . it is too difficult."

For several moments they stood staring at the Ronin in wonder. Then Kristina motioned for them all to return to the outer portions of the cavern. "Now," she murmured, "you can understand the drawing better. It's an interpretation of this pattern. I've tried to stress the dimensionality of the pattern by the use of color."

As the three of them turned to go, the Ronin called out in a hoarse whisper. "Wait! This unit . . . this unit cannot move!"

Kim stepped to his side and looked into his eyes. "What do you mean you can't move?"

"This unit . . . no, the Mind Brothers this unit carries cannot . . . no, do not wish to leave the junction point. They wish to stay for something, something that will come sometime."

Kristina came over and looked deeply into the Ronin's eyes. "Yes," she nodded. "Yes, I can feel it. The power of the pattern affects the Mind Brothers. That last smoothstone must have completed some circuit. I know there's still one missing. I can feel its absence, but maybe the pattern is already complete enough to affect the Mushin.

"But why," she wondered aloud, "should it affect them? And how does it do it?"

The Earthman took one of the Ronin's arms and gently

turned the man until he was facing the entrance to the cavern. "There. Now Kim and I are going to move you slowly toward the entrance, away from the pattern. Try to bring your Mind Brothers with you."

Slowly, the three of them moved, the Ronin rigid and pulling slightly back as they walked. Suddenly, with a slight cry, he went limp and collapsed. "Gods!" Kim said. "Let's get him out of here!"

Back in the main cave, Kristina worked over the limp form of the Ronin, trying to bring him back to consciousness. Finally, as she held some pungent herbs beneath his nose, he groaned and began to stir. As his eyes opened they were blank, but they rapidly filled with fear.

"This unit . . . the Brothers . . . empty . . . alone . . . this unit . . ."

"Take it easy, Erik," Kim said. "You're all right. We got you out of the cavern."

"Out . . . Mind Brothers stayed . . . this unit is empty . . . this unit is hollow . . . Totality is . . . ah . . . ah . . ." With a slight cry the Ronin fainted again.

"Kim," Dunn said, looking quizzically at the young woman, "what happened to *your* Mind Brothers? They're gone and so are his. I can't feel Mushin anywhere around here."

The young woman concentrated for a moment, then looked at the Earthman and the older woman with wonder in her eyes. "He's right! I can't feel any Mind Brothers! Both mine and Erik's are gone!"

Kristina looked thoughtful. "No. I don't think they're gone. I think they're just caught in the field of the smoothstones."

The two looked at her. "What in the name of Kuvaz do you mean?" Dunn asked.

She looked pensive. "I'm not too sure. I think what I mean is that the Mushin somehow seem to respond to the energy pattern that the smoothstones create. You see, in real life, on the face of Kensho, the smoothstones are scattered about at great distances from each other. Here, though, they are close together, so the energy field they generate is concentrated and more powerful. That's probably the only reason we can even sense it. A single stone isn't strong enough for us to notice and the whole mass of them all across the planet are too far apart to create more than a very tenuous pattern of energy. It's probably the same for the Mushin."

"Why would they affect the Mushin? What kind of connection could there be between smoothstones and Mind Brothers?" Kim asked. "And what's happened to Erik?"

"The first two questions I have no way of answering, for I know as little as you. As to the last one, though, I think I have a pretty good idea. You see, the Ronin are a very special type of human being. When the Mushin struck at First Touch, most of us assumed there were only two types of responses. One group, the group that lacked any form of mind control, went mad and died in murderous insanity. The other, those who did have some kind of control, managed to escape the Madness. It was these latter, some ten percent of all those who had come from Earth on the Pilgrimage, that Yamada gathered together and managed to save.

"But there was a third type of response to the Mushin. If the first group had an undisciplined sense of self and fell easy prey to the Mushin, and the second group were able to submerge their sense of self so that the Mushin had nothing to attack, the third group was innately capable of transcending their limited sense of self and identifying with a much larger entity, that is with Totality. They didn't go insane. They simply became unsane. They didn't become targets for the Mind Leeches because they merged with them. At that instant, Totality expanded and changed. It became the Mushin . . . and a group of human minds, the Ronin.

"Ever since that time the two have really been one. I think that what we have considered the 'calming down' of the Mushin and the Ronin has actually been nothing more than the result of the growing accommodation between the two, the greater integration of the one into the other.

"What Erik is experiencing is being cut off from that unity for the first time. He is alone, utterly. I rather imagine that would take some getting used to."

Kim looked down at the Ronin's thin face. "What will happen to him?"

Kristina shrugged. "He could go mad, but somehow, from what I've seen of him, I doubt he will. He's always seemed to me to be relatively independent in his relationship to Totality. The shock will be terrible, but I believe he'll survive it. I'll give him some calming draughts to ease him over the initial shock."

Kim looked up at Dunn and saw that the Earthman was staring off into space. "Dunn?"

Dunn's faraway look cleared, and his gaze fastened on her. "Kim," he said quietly, "I have to get back to First Touch. We all do."

The young woman looked at him blankly. "Back to First Touch? Why?"

"Because that's where the Way-Farer will be. And Josh and Myali. Kim, Kristina, we've got to get back there and let them know about this thing with the smoothstones and the Mushin."

"Why?" Kim asked again, her gaze still uncomprehending.

The Earthman frowned in concentration. "I'm not one hundred percent sure myself. I just have a feeling that this is very important. Josh always said that he felt the Mushin were the key to defending Kensho from the Earth Fleet that's on the way. I don't know whether he's right or not, but I've got a hunch this piece of information that Kristina's discovered is very important. Erik's part of it, too."

"He won't be ready to travel for at least a week, Dunn," Kristina said.

"Can't we just have ourselves Snatched?" he asked.

"Of course!" Kim answered. "We'll just call your friend Josh and he can . . ." Her voice ran down.

"What's the matter?" Dunn asked.

"We can't call," Kim answered. "Our Mushin, our Mind Brothers are in the pattern. We don't have any."

"Can't we just get some more?"

"Way out here? Not likely. The Mushin cluster near human habitation. There isn't even a 'stead in this area. Closest one must be a good three days' travel from here."

"Damn. Then we'll have to let them out of the pattern, move the smoothstones and set them free."

"No," Kristina said, "that isn't a good idea. Once the pattern is set, changing it takes a good deal of energy. Any disruption releases energy as well. The pattern in there is pretty powerful right now. The Mushin in it seem to actually add to its strength. I'm not too sure what would happen to us if we broke the pattern and set them loose. We might not survive it."

Dunn looked at her in stunned surprise. "You mean the damn thing is dangerous?"

She nodded. "I think so. It's very concentrated. Kim and I might make it, Dunn, but I'm not sure you would. Nor am I certain about Erik in his current state. No. I fear that if you want to get to First Touch, you're going to have to walk there."

For a few moments, he quietly considered what the older woman had said. Then he nodded. "All right, if that's the way it is then the sooner we get started, the better. How soon will Erik be ready to travel?"

Kristina considered. "Ummmmm. Say a week or two."

"Fine. Then in the meantime Kim and I will make preparations for the trip. Uh . . . if possible I'd really like you to come along. It could be very important."

She and Kim passed a considering look between them. The older woman frowned slightly as she spoke. "It could be even more important than you realize, Dunn."

"What do you mean?"

"Well, in our journeys around the area, Kim and Erik and I have noticed a rather disturbing increase in the number of Ronin bands in the vicinity."

"Ronin? How many?"

"Hard to tell exactly," Kim answered. "Could be as few as two or three or as many as six. Their tracks get confused at times."

The Earthman's mouth dropped open. "Six bands? By the Power, what could be drawing that many to this area? Why, there's nothing here, no 'steads, no . . ." He stopped and looked at Kristina, a sudden question on his face.

She nodded slowly. "Yes, it's quite possible that the

pattern in the cavern is drawing them. Perhaps their Mushin sense it. I don't really know.

"Whatever it is, though, getting past them to First Touch might be a little more of a problem than any of us had bargained for. I've got a feeling you're going to need all the help you can get."

Dunn looked slowly at the two of them, then down at the still form of the Ronin. "We've got to try," he murmured. "Don't ask me why, but I know we've got to try."

❧ Chapter 20 ❧

Dunn stumbled and gave a slight grunt of pain. The leg was getting weaker and more painful with every step he took. Kristina had watched him trudge along all day and she had seen his exhaustion grow by the hour. She knew she would have to call a halt pretty soon. Neither Dunn nor Erik could travel much further.

Yet both of them were doing much better than she had dared to hope. When she had first seen the Earthman lying there on his pallet, with his leg mangled and swollen, she had been sure he wasn't going to make it. And when they had had to move him to the cave, she had been positive it was his death warrant.

Amazingly, the man had survived. When he had finally opened his eyes and looked around the cave, when she had heard the flat hopelessness of his voice and seen the depths of soul-shaking confusion that filled his eyes, she had once again despaired of his recovery. His body had fought heroically to beat the infection. Would a lack of will bring about his defeat after all?

But again, she had marveled to see him come back, inch by inch, from the edge. It had begun one day when she had come out of her inner sanctum to find he had dragged himself to the mouth of the cave and was looking out at the sky. His gaze had been steady, calm, and considering, almost as if the sun and clouds had given him something important to think about.

And think he obviously had. He never mentioned what was going through his mind to anyone, but he would often

157

sit for hours in silent concentration as though working
through complex and difficult problems.

Slowly but surely he had changed. The light of life had
come back into his eyes. He began to talk to others and
respond in a normal way. Still, there were always long
periods of intense thinking when he would simply ignore
the existence of everyone for hours on end. He always
came out of those sessions with a slight, deprecating smile
on his lips as if to beg everyone's pardon for his absence.
She often wondered what he thought about at those times,
but she had a good idea it had to do with the problems
Kim had told her he was struggling with. People didn't
usually take to Wandering for light reasons. She felt sure
he would tell them all when he was good and ready.

Erik was improving as well. At first the Ronin had been
almost comatose. He would have starved to death if they
hadn't been there to care for him. The black-clad man had
turned totally inward, it seemed. He had simply lain on his
side, in a loose fetal position, his eyes open but unfocused,
his breath light and regular.

Gradually, he had let the world in. But he had changed
dramatically. The Ronin who had once moved with the
grace and fluidity of a wild animal, now blundered about
like a man in a dream.

Dunn stumbled again and went down on one knee. He
cursed lightly and tried to struggle upright before they all
came to a halt. Erik, whom Kim was more or less leading,
tripped and nearly fell on his face. Kristina looked at both
their faces. Dunn was positively gray and his expression
was pinched with pain. Erik's face was slack and exhausted.

The condition of the two men made her decide it was
time to stop, even though there were a good five hours of
travel time left before night began to fall. She realized that
if there was to be a second day to this journey, the first had
best be cut short.

Dunn sat and stared gloomily at his leg. Erik sat and
stared emptily at nothing. Kim came and sat next to the
older woman. "Well," the younger woman sighed, "at
least I can't complain about the breakneck speed."

The Earthman looked up and scowled. "Guess I was a

little more out of practice in walking than I realized. Just need some time to get used to it again. I'll do better tomorrow."

Kristina smiled slightly. "No, you won't do better tomorrow. You'll do worse. By morning, you're going to be so sore and stiff you'll hardly be able to move, much less walk. You've been using your good leg all day to compensate for the bad one. Both are exhausted. It'll be two days at best before you start to make much of an improvement in your speed, Dunn. So, until then, we just take it easy. Besides, Erik is just as bad a traveler as you are right about now."

"Will he ever get any better?" Kim asked, casting a worried glance toward the Ronin. "He doesn't seem to have made much progress in the last week and a half. He still just sits there and stares off—"

"He's a lot better, Kim," Dunn interrupted. "At least he can dress and feed himself! At first, he couldn't even do that!"

"Yes," Kristina nodded, "Dunn's right. He's steadily improving. Today I saw him looking directly at things several times. He clearly recognized them for what they were."

She sighed. "Don't forget he's had a rather traumatic experience. It would be like one of us suddenly becoming deaf, dumb, and blind at the same time. Only a lot worse because it's all taken place inside his head and cut him off from the very thing which has defined him since he was a baby." She shook her head. "I find it hard to even imagine what he's going through. In a way, it must be like growing up all over again."

Dunn looked down at the ground and said softly, "I have a pretty good idea of what it's like for him. They didn't tear his mind apart like they did mine, but I imagine the result's pretty much the same."

"No," Kristina answered, "I don't think so. They actually ripped apart what already existed in your mind and destroyed it. In Erik's case, nothing was destroyed. Everything that was originally there is still there. The only thing he's missing is the central organizing force that made it all make sense."

Kim looked up at her, puzzlement showing on her face. "Do you mean the Mushin?"

"More than the Mushin. I mean Totality, the unity that made everything cohere. Erik was a part of the whole, a unit in Totality. Everything he did, everything he experienced, was filtered through Totality and Totality structured it and gave it meaning within the context of everything else Totality experienced. You might say that Totality was the interface between his mind and the stimulus he received. With that gone, he must construct some new way of dealing with stimuli, some new way of filtering and giving them meaning."

The Earthman looked interested. "Are you saying that Erik had a self all along? That his self was really Totality? That's what it sounds like to me, anyway. I mean, isn't what you're describing one of the functions of the self?"

"In a way, I guess it is," the older woman responded. "Though I'm not sure that a self is necessary to structure stimuli. After all, an amoeba can deal successfully with data from its environment. But, yes, I think at the very least we might say that the self is a *result* of the interaction between mind and stimuli. Therefore, in all probability, it does occupy a place between the two. You should remember, however, that any adequate description of self would have to be a good deal more complex than that."

Dunn looked thoughtful. "Yes, I know. I've been giving it a lot of thought lately." He chuckled, looking ruefully down at his leg. "I haven't had much else to do and there's nothing like having a creature try to eat you alive to make you do some heavy thinking. Also, that's the main reason I went Wandering in the first place."

Kristina nodded. "Kim and Erik told me a good deal about you and your dilemma."

"Yeh. Only I'm not too sure it's really such a big dilemma anymore."

"What do you mean, Dunn?" Kim asked, her eyes lighting up with interest. "Have you found your sense of self?"

"Not exactly," the Earthman admitted. "I'm really not too sure it's even possible to pin it down and study it. Let me give you an example of what I mean." Unexpectedly, he whistled a few bars of a song he remembered from many years ago on Earth. Finished, he grinned at the two women sheepishly. "Sorry. Not much of a musician, but it makes my point.

"That song, now. What is it that makes it a coherent whole? You can't halt it at any point and say, 'That's it, that's the song.' If you do, all you have is that note, that instant of sound you just completed. The rest is either gone or yet to come.

"The music consists of a whole group of notes and the empty spaces between them. It doesn't inhere in any one of them, or even in any group of them. Nor is music a musical score, a bunch of symbols written down on paper. That score can be used by musicians to re-create the music, but by itself it's not the music.

"The music isn't the musicians, their instruments, or their performance, either. Almost every time a piece of music is performed, it comes out differently, in subtle ways.

"No, music isn't any of these things. As soon as you try to examine a piece of music it simply dissolves right in front of your eyes. It falls into tiny, seemingly unrelated and almost unrelatable pieces.

"Yet," Dunn said with a small smile, "music, like the little song I just whistled, does exist. And it exists as a coherent, understandable whole.

"How can that be? How can something which is meaningless when taken apart have significance when put together?" He shrugged. "I thought a long time about that because that's exactly the problem I encountered when I tried to study my sense of self. It dissolved as I tried to pin it down, just the way a piece of music does when you take it apart."

Dunn shifted to ease the pain in his leg. He sighed slightly. "Yeh. I worried about that a long time after I met Erik. Then the music analogy helped me realize something. If you don't mind, I'll stick with it a bit longer.

"Music exists in the process of happening. Its distinctive character, its very coherency and being come from its being performed. Instantaneousness is its very essence. Each note leads to the next and builds on what has already passed. The memory provides a bridge that makes the whole cohere, but of course memory isn't music."

"But Dunn," Kim protested, "you can study music by looking at its parts. You can separate out themes, combinations, counterpoint, harmony, all those things."

The Earthman nodded in agreement. "Sure. You can take music apart to study its structure, even to figure out how it works. But none of what you study is the music as a whole. That doesn't exist in any meaningful sense until it is in the process of being played.

"The more I thought about it, the more I realized that the self is very much like a piece of music. First of all, it's a whole and has a quality not possessed by any of its many parts. Second, all the parts are interrelated, and changing any one of them changes all of them and creates a slightly different whole. Third, you can't separate parts from the whole without changing their nature. That's very important, because what I had been trying to do was to isolate things and separate them from the whole in my search for some kind of concrete proof of the self. That was a mistake, a fallacy in the Ronin's argument. I was assuming that the parts were somehow more real than the whole. I was like a man studying a building by taking it apart brick by brick and then after I had it all apart wondering what had happened to the building I wanted to study.

"What I had been searching for was some hidden 'thing,' some kind of 'core' that was the self. But the self isn't revealed in that way. Rather than being revealed in repose, in some 'thisness,' it's present only in action, in the process of acting. The self isn't a body, it's a constant happening, an endless becoming.

"Now, the self isn't *pure* change and becoming, of course. It has coherency, individuality if you will. My self is very different from yours. Yours is different from someone else's. Furthermore, there's a consistency through time to a self. It doesn't totally change, under ordinary circumstances, in an instant of time. Again, like a piece of music, it has themes, melodies, harmonies that give it individual character.

"On the other hand, the self is clearly not pure stability or being. As I've already said, it's something that is in process of happening, like a piece of music. It's something which must become in order to be.

"If the self is constantly becoming, it's constantly changing. It's always associated with the stream of experience, with the stimuli we receive through our senses from the external, and our own internal, world. One can't discover an experience that's neither yours nor mine, that is, one not associated with some self. The presence of the self is constant, its permanence essential in order to make sense of experience.

"Yet it changes, grows, develops. It's not ready-made, but created every instant by what we do and what we experience. Its coherency is not a preordained substantial one. It comes into being as it acts, its substance is its process of becoming. It builds on what has been to form what will be. It's not merely memory of the past but memory hurled into the future through the instant-wide opening of present experience. The past never entirely disappears, just as in a piece of music, but it may be reinterpreted and change its very meaning in the future."

Dunn sat silent for a moment. Kim and Kristina shared his silence, trying to absorb all he had said. He shifted his weight, wincing at his already tightening muscles. Eventually, he found a more comfortable position and began to speak once more.

"The Dunn who Bishop Thwait tried to destroy remembered a few of the things he had learned during his training, things that they missed or else that just weren't important enough to erase. There was a scientist on Earth, long before Kuvaz and the whole Readjustment, a man called Heisenberg. He posited something called an Indeterminacy Principle. Basically, what he said was that you can't observe things like subatomic particles without changing them through the act of observation. On a broader scale, what that meant was that there really was no line separating subject from object, that subject in the process of studying object mixed itself with object, or at least affected it, in a way which changed it and made it no longer independent of subject."

Kristina nodded. "Yes. I found much the same thing. The line between subject and object is an artificial one.

Self is part of all, indeed has no meaning without all. Yes, I agree with your ancient Earth scientist."

"Well," Dunn continued, "self is very like a subatomic particle. The process of examining it changes it. You can't isolate it any more than you can isolate part of a piece of music and claim you have the whole. Examining it is an experience, and it's experience which forms the self. Hence, examining it changes it. You can't pin it down because the thing you're pinning is the thing doing the pinning. It's like trying to lift yourself off the ground with your own hands.

"When I realized all of these things, I suddenly discovered that my own problem, my loss of self, my inability to find my own self, simply dissolved. I have as much a self as anyone does. The experience of the destruction of my 'old' self is one of the bases for my 'new' self. Everything I have experienced since then has changed and developed that self. I'm no more a partial creature than anyone else. I'm a whole. I'm me. I have a self as complete and as detailed as any in existence.

"I've done my Wandering. I've found the answer that was right there all the time. I can go home now." He smiled gently at the two women.

Kristina smiled back. "Yes, Dunn. You can go home now. Because now home is everywhere."

Kim smiled, too. But her smile was brief, overshadowed by the deep considering look that filled her eyes. It was clear that the things Dunn had said were giving her a great deal to think about.

In thoughtful silence, the three of them began to make camp.

⑨ Chapter 21 ⑨

For the next two days they traveled slowly east in order to reach the narrow plain that lay between the range of hills and the swamps that bordered the sea to the east. Kristina explained that although this didn't get them any closer to their goal, it would offer an easier path for Dunn and Erik once they got there. In addition, that route was less traveled by Ronin and they had been running across a disturbing abundance of signs of sizable bands of the black-clad killers.

Dunn was walking more easily now, though he still tired early in the day. At best he was good for five hours of slow travel. Erik was also improving, somewhat more slowly than Dunn, but getting better nonetheless. He generally responded with short monosyllabic answers when spoken to directly, and his awareness of what was happening around him was growing. The Ronin still remained listless and awkward, however. It seemed as if his personality, his drive, his spirit had been sucked from him when the Mushin he carried were trapped in the field in Kristina's cave.

At the moment, Erik, Dunn, and Kim were resting in a narrow valley between two hills before struggling up the next slope. Kristina had told them that they were almost out of the hills now and that soon the going would be much easier. The older woman had gone ahead to look over the trail and to check for Ronin.

Suddenly, unexpectedly, Kristina appeared before them. Damn, the Earthman thought, she moves like a shadow in the woods! He was about to comment on her

165

ability when he saw the expression on her face. "Ronin," she said in a soft whisper, "just the other side of the hill, south about half a mile and heading north. They should pass us by without seeing us."

"How many?" Kim asked, copying her whisper.

The strange look on the older woman's face intensified. "I'd estimate about fifteen to twenty."

They looked at her with undisguised amazement. "But," Dunn protested weakly, "that's impossible. They never travel in packs of more than five or six. Everybody knows that."

"Everybody except the Ronin on the other side of this hill," Kristina replied. She gave Dunn a quick smile. "Sorry. I don't mean to be sarcastic. I find it as hard to believe as the rest of you." She turned her gaze to Erik. "Erik, do you understand what I just said?"

The Ronin returned her gaze, clearly struggling to focus his attention and concentrate. "Yes," he nodded slowly. "Yes, I understand."

"Good. Listen carefully. We've been running across the trails of many Ronin parties, all heading north. Many, many parties. And all of them are larger than usual. Kim, how many did you figure were in that one we spotted the tracks of yesterday afternoon?"

The young woman considered a moment. "Well, at the time I said seven or eight, but I really felt there were more. Just couldn't accept the idea, though, so I lowered the number. Hmmmm. I guess I'd say twelve to fifteen considering what you've just reported."

Kristina nodded. "That's what I estimate. So far, in the three days we've been traveling, and we haven't exactly covered large amounts of ground, I've counted the trails of no less than five groups. Five. That's more than you generally see in this area in a year." She turned back to Erik. "Do you have any idea what in Jerome's name is going on?"

Sweat was standing out on the Ronin's forehead from the strength of his effort to concentrate. "No. This . . . this . . . no. Strange. Not know. No. Too many. Ronin don't do. Not know." With a sigh that was almost a groan, he lowered his glance toward the ground, his shoulders slumping with exhaustion. "Strange," he mumbled. "Strange."

"And damn dangerous," Kim muttered. "Gods, Kristina, we can barely defend ourselves against four Ronin. But against fifteen or twenty—"

"Damn," Dunn interrupted, "we can't even run from them. We'll have to have someone out front from now on to scout as we go. That'll slow us down even more. Why in the name of Kuvaz are they doing it? What does it mean? Have you got any ideas, Kristina?"

The older woman shook her head. "Nothing worth mentioning. I've never heard or seen anything like it. Ronin simply don't behave that way."

"Hmmm," Dunn mused. "You know, I've got a feeling that you people really know damn little of how Ronin behave. Erik, for example, contradicts everything I've ever been told about Ronin. And how many times have I heard one of the Fathers in the 'hood talk about how the Ronin have been changing over the years? Yet no one that I know of has ever paid much attention to them other than to figure out new ways to fight and kill them."

"But, Dunn," Kim protested, "they kill us. They're our enemies. They—"

"All the more reason to know as much as possible about them," he replied. "Besides, I see something about them that I guess all the rest of you here on Kensho are just too close to see. They're as human as you are, Kim. They came on the same ship, from the same planet. Oh, I grant they've changed a lot since the disaster at First Touch, but so have the rest of you. Kensho has changed the race, Kim. And to be honest with you, as an outsider, you and the Ronin are a lot more alike than either of you are like Earthmen."

Kristina gave him a thoughtful look. "Your ideas are interesting, Dunn. If we ever get to First Touch, I think they should be investigated more thoroughly. Right now though, our major problem is getting there. The plan of a scout out front is a good one. Kim and I will trade off in that job. Now," she rose and looked down at the three of them, "I imagine the Ronin I saw have passed by. I'll take first turn at scout duty. I'll stay about five minutes ahead of the rest of you and come back immediately if anything strange turns up. Just to be safe, it would be best to pause at each ridgetop and check the lay of the land before you cross. Let's go."

"How much farther in these damn hills?" Dunn grumped.

The older woman smiled. "Sometime tomorrow afternoon we should reach the flatter area of the plain. It's narrow in places, Dunn. You remember that. Now and then, we'll still have to head back into the hills to pass around the swamp."

"Fine," the Earthman replied with a slight shiver. "Fine. I've got absolutely no objection to going around the swamp. Even if it means climbing mountains!"

Late the next afternoon, true to Kristina's prediction, they walked through the last hills and came to the plain. At this point, and for about a day's journey north, it was fairly wide. Then it gradually narrowed as the swamp spread westward. Eventually, perhaps three or four days north, they would have to enter the hills again.

The next morning dawned cloudy and with more than a hint of a storm in the air. They decided to travel as far as they could and take shelter only when the storm was imminent. As they had agreed, they sent a scout out ahead. Although they weren't in an area the Ronin usually traveled in, they had seen too much evidence of a large movement of the black-clad killers to feel comfortable no matter where they were. Kim took first turn.

As she walked through the thick woods, Kim's mind ranged over all that had happened in the recent past. A lot of it still didn't make any sense to her. The smoothstones and the pattern in Kristina's cave were an utter mystery to her, as was the trapping of the Mushin within the pattern. Dunn's recovery and his seeming peace of mind were, despite his explanations, almost as miraculous as the utter collapse of Erik. It seemed quite obvious to the young woman that the Ronin had been correct in saying he had no self. If he had one, his collapse wouldn't have been so total.

But then, if he had no self, how could she account for his slow recovery? Every day, the black-clad man was becoming more and more coherent. He would answer in complete sentences now. And he noticed almost everything that happened around him. He was moving like a normal person, though not with anything like his former grace and fluidity. Yet, she admitted, he still seemed hollow, as though there were a large empty space somewhere at his center. And there was a haunted quality to his eyes . . .

She shrugged. He was getting better. Maybe that, too, would pass with time. She liked the Ronin. Hopefully he would once again be the person she had known.

Where did all that leave her? Nowhere. She didn't feel as though she was one step closer to solving her own problem. The things Kristina had said interested her a great deal, since they implied that one didn't have to lose one's self, only to transcend it, indeed to expand it to include the entire universe! That was a bit much for her to deal with, but it was an intriguing idea well worth consideration. If she could achieve that . . .

She stopped dead in her tracks and froze. There had been a movement up ahead to the left. Slowly, she sank into a crouching position, peering through the dense underbrush. There. And there. Movement. Could it be some kind of animal?

Kim sank lower as the bushes rustled much nearer. She heard a soft call and a form appeared in the gloom. Not an animal. A man. A Ronin!

Trying to control her panic and alarm, she carefully swept the area with her eyes. One there, another there, at least two more there, the one near, the one who called back, perhaps two or three more she couldn't see. She had to get back and tell the others! They'd walk right into this pack if they weren't warned!

She was about to turn and crawl away when she heard a noise behind and to her right. Another one! Behind her! She was surrounded! She bent lower until she was virtually lying on the forest floor. One noise, she realized, and ten Ronin would be on her, hacking her to death with their swords. She didn't stand a chance against numbers like that, especially when they could come at her from all sides. She saw something move and realized it was her own hand. It was shaking.

Death, she thought. I've never been this close to it. Except in that pass. That was close, but the odds were better then.

She suppressed a whimper of terror. I don't want to die. Not yet. Not like this. Silent tears began to run down her face.

Anger flared up. Damn! Why am I such a coward? I'm afraid of everything! The Ronin, losing my self, everything. I won't yield to this fear! I won't!

I can't, she suddenly realized. If I do, I'm dead for sure. And so are the others.

The others! Oh Gods! They were just a few minutes behind, depending on her to warn them of danger. And she couldn't move for fear of being discovered and killed. How could she warn them? There had to be a way. There had to—

Suddenly, hopelessly, she knew what she had to do. The very thought of it momentarily paralyzed her with terror. She forced herself to relax. No sense in waiting, she thought. I might as well get it over with. Good-bye Erik, Dunn, Kristina. You're the best friends I've ever had. I'm glad I had a chance to know you. Too bad I couldn't have found what I was looking for.

With that, she leapt to her feet, gave the loudest shout she could, and ran for all she was worth. She headed northwest.

They heard Kim's shout. There was a brief silence, then an incredible chorus of yipping, baying cries. Stunned, they all stood and stared at each other.

"Damn," Dunn said softly. "Ronin."

Kristina's face was white. "Kim and Ronin," she corrected. "They're after her. A lot of them."

Erik's whole body was tense with understanding. "Kim, yes. Ronin chase her. We must go, now. We must help her."

The older woman looked at the two men. "She did it to save us, to draw them off. They must have surprised her and she couldn't get back to warn us in time. This is her warning, her way to save us."

"We go. Now." Erik began to move off.

Kristina turned to Dunn. "Earthman, go to First Touch. You have something to tell the Way-Farer and the Council, I can sense it. It has something to do with my smoothstones and the Mushin. Perhaps it is as important as you think. I can't know that. But it could be. So go. We will go help Kim and catch up. If we don't, keep going on our own, don't waste Kim's sacrifice. Go."

"Bullshit," Dunn growled. "I'm going with you. Kim's my friend, too. Goddamn Way-Farer can just wait. Let's go!"

Kim ran as she had never run before. Behind came the screaming and crashing of her pursuers. She sucked in huge gulps of air, trying to drag as much energy as she could into her body. As she ran, her eyes strained ahead, looking for someplace to make a stand. She knew death was inevitable, but she wanted to hold the Ronin as long as she could to give the others as much time as possible to make their escape.

Suddenly she saw it. A huge ko tree ahead and to her right. It had to be at least ten feet in diameter! A giant. One she could trust her back to. She almost grinned as she heard the Ronin yelping. More than one of them wouldn't ever yelp again in the very near future. She wouldn't die alone!

She reached the tree a good fifty paces ahead of the first of the black-clad killers. A strange thought came to her as she saw him joined by two others that came crashing through the underbrush to come up short as they saw their prey at bay. Where do they get all that black cloth to make their robes from? They must make it themselves. The thought of a Ronin at a loom weaving cloth was so incongruous it made her laugh out loud.

The laugh clearly surprised the Ronin. Two more joined the others. Then an additional three showed up. That made a total of eight. She heard a noise in the forest and realized that there were still more on their way. No hope.

She felt the pressure of their Mushin. With a sudden

twist of her mind, she reached out and captured some of them for herself. She needed the energy the Mind Brothers provided. For the first time since hers had been trapped in the design, she realized how much she had missed them.

The Ronin were all there now. There were eleven of them. They had sized up the situation and were spread out in a semicircle, slowly approaching her. She picked one out, one that was a little in front of the others in his eagerness to kill. He would be the first to attack, the first she had to stop. Each blow had to be fatal, she realized. There wouldn't be time for second strikes. So be it.

She was ready. Ready to die. Strangely, it felt good. All indecision, all doubt was swept away. She was calmer than she had ever been in her life.

The Ronin she had picked leapt at her with a shriek, his sword flashing up and back for a blow. With a smile on her face, she stepped forward to meet his attack.

⑤ Chapter 22 ⑤

"NO!"

The sheer volume and authority of the shout stopped everyone, both the Ronin and Kim, in their tracks. Hands holding weapons froze where they were, hanging in space. Mouths, open to shriek and shout, became silent, gaping holes. Every head turned slowly to seek the source of the commanding cry.

What they discovered was another Ronin. The hood of his black robe had fallen back, revealing shockingly light blond hair, glowing blue eyes, and a sharp, hawklike face divided by a beak of a nose. The short, wiry frame was tensed and ready, the chest heaving to draw in air; he was in complete control.

"No," Erik said again, more softly this time but with the same intense demand in his voice. "All units will cease this attack."

As one, the Ronin turned their eyes to a dark-haired giant who stood near the rear of the pack. This one slowly turned to face Erik. "Who seeks to command this group of units?" he asked in a deep, growling voice.

"I am Erik," came the proud reply, "and this human woman is a friend of mine. No unit will touch her."

"You have no say here. You do not even carry Mind Brothers."

Erik drew himself up to his full height and placed his hand on the hilt of his sword. "I challenge for right of He-Who-Carries-Most."

A murmur broke out among the Ronin and they lowered their swords, despite the fact that Dunn and Kristina

173

arrived at that exact moment. "You challenge?" asked the dark-haired giant. "Fagh! You are an empty unit! You do not even carry Mind Brothers. How can such a barren one hope to challenge a unit so filled with Brothers as this unit? You shall die, fool, and then we will kill all these humans!"

Erik drew his sword and smiled at the huge Ronin. "Barren unit? Soon I shall have all your Mind Brothers. Do you not recognize me? Ah, of course not! Without my Mind Brothers you cannot share in my mind, cannot recognize which unit I am." He swept the group of Ronin with a cold eye. "Soon enough you will all know me. I am Erik!" Without another word he flowed smoothly forward toward the man he was challenging.

The two circled, each carefully taking the measure of his opponent. Kim was amazed to see that Erik was moving as smoothly as he always had. The jerky, puppetlike movements were gone. The Ronin was once again the catlike killing machine of the past.

Surprisingly, the huge Ronin moved just as smoothly. She watched him with a judging eye. A good, confident fighter. He had the reach on Erik by at least two inches. It would be hard to tell how fast the man was until the actual fighting began.

Erik feinted a head cut and the other countered with a light block that turned into a thrust for the throat. Erik brushed that aside with a counter to the wrists which the other blocked easily. Satisfied that neither of them was an easy kill, they circled once again.

With his eyes glued to the action, Dunn asked Kristina a question in a low voice. "What is this 'He-Who-Carries' business?" She shook her head and replied softly, "Don't know. But by the sound of it, I think it must mean that groups of Ronin have some kind of leadership position. There's so much we don't know."

The two Ronin met again in a swift exchange of blows. Dunn marveled at the speed and skill of both men. Either would finish me off in a single pass, he admitted. I sure am glad Erik was in a peaceful mood when we first met! The two killers parted again, neither having been able to gain the opening he needed. They were panting now, and despite the coolness of the day, they were beginning to sweat.

Kim looked up at the sky. It could rain at any minute, she realized. Would that help or hurt their chances? She cautiously took the knife from her leg scabbard and stuck it in her belt in back. Measuring the distance to the two nearest Ronin, she calculated that she could probably drop both of them before they could react. Especially if they stayed as involved with the finish of the fight as they were with its unfolding.

I'm assuming Erik will lose, she thought. She looked quickly over at Dunn and saw he had his hand on his sword's hilt. Kristina was equally ready. We're all thinking the same thing, she told herself. If Erik loses, we have to strike instantly. Even then, the odds aren't too good.

But what if Erik wins? Could that be just as bad? Would he be able to control the Ronin and keep them from falling on the humans and slaughtering them? She wasn't at all sure exactly what He-Who-Carries-Most meant and how much control over the others it involved. And what would happen when Erik was carrying Mushin again? Would he revert back to his original Ronin nature and join the others in the killing? The only thing to do was to hope for the best and prepare for the worst.

The two Ronin leapt at each other again. Erik faked a wrist cut and flipped it up for a throat jab. The other killer dodged and slashed toward Erik's side. The blade sliced through his robe as he twisted and leapt away from the blow. As he jumped, he swept his own sword up and ripped into his opponent's shoulder.

Both stepped back, panting and heaving with the exertion of their combat. Erik could feel the warm blood trickling down his side. The blow had hit flesh, but it couldn't have gone very deep because the blood was oozing rather than gushing. He could see the spreading stain on the black-haired giant's robe marking where his own slash had gotten through.

Despite his wound, Erik felt utterly exhilarated. His mind was as clear and deep as a pool of forest water. It seemed to him that he could actually feel what his opponent was going to do an instant before he was going to do it. Like now, that slight swelling of the neck meant he was going to attack again.

The giant stepped in and went for his wrists, changing to a throat thrust at the last moment. Erik knocked it aside easily and cut quickly for the head. His opponent blocked and stepped back. Erik rocked back as though to disengage. The other man dropped the point of his sword ever so slightly and began to shift his weight onto his left foot so he could move to the right.

Rather than stepping back, though, Erik shifted forward again and attacked with a head cut. His opponent realized what was happening, raised his sword to block and began to shift his weight back onto his right foot.

Erik threw his right foot out and stepped deep to the other man's left side, bringing his sword down from the head strike in a slash across the chest. It was too late for the dark-haired Ronin to counter. He was off balance, his weight mostly on his right foot, his sword coming down, but not down far enough. Erik twisted to his right as his blade bit, giving his blow even more energy. He followed up his deep right step with an equally deep left step which bore his body and blade along with even greater momentum. The razor-sharp steel sliced through flesh and bone like an ordinary blade moving through water.

The giant Ronin grunted. For a second he stood still as Erik passed him, then he turned again, his sword ready to strike once more. He opened his mouth as if to speak. A fountain of red gore burst forth from his lips and slowly, slowly he fell forward, his sword tumbling gently to the forest floor from fingers that no longer cared to hold it.

Everyone, including the humans, was too stunned to move. Erik slowly lowered his sword and opened his mind to the Mind Brothers that swarmed around the dying man. With one incredible gulp, he took them all under control. Then he whirled and glared at the other Ronin. "Put away your swords," he commanded. "No one is to touch these humans. They are mine."

The other Ronin were so disoriented by what had happened that they complied without even thinking. Erik turned to Kim, his face tense, his voice tight. "Get out of here, all of you. I don't know how long I can hold them. It will take a while before I can gain dominance. Get out, all of you. Now!"

Kim nodded and gestured to Dunn and Kristina. They had heard Erik and understood. They moved quickly to her side. Then the three of them turned and moved swiftly off into the woods, heading north.

Erik watched them go and then turned to face the other Ronin. "Is there any unit so foolish as to challenge my right to He-Who-Carries-Most?"

They muttered softly and exchanged glances from beneath their brows. One of them finally spoke for the others. "No. These units are in acceptance. It is the will of Totality."

Erik nodded and smiled. "Yes, it is the will of Totality." He closed his eyes for a moment and let his consciousness spread out, following the connections between the Mushin he carried and those carried by the others in his band.

After familiarizing himself with all the patterns, he let his mind range wider, reaching out through the Mind Brothers' links to those farther away. He detected a small group moving north at a rapid pace. That would be Kim. He smiled. There was a large group further west, two southwest, one dead south, and another just ahead to the northeast. Many groups. Far too many. It wasn't normal. He probed deeper.

Where were they all heading? There didn't seem to be any firm destination in mind, just a general intention of heading northward. Northward? To what? A vague picture. A place of much eating after a long hunger. What place could that be? he wondered.

Then it hit him. First Touch and Base Camp! The place where men and Mushin had first met on Kensho! Where the slaughter had taken place that had so nearly ended the human race's stay on the planet. And the place where the Way-Farer and the Council spent most of their time. It was also the destination of Kim, Dunn, and Kristina, his friends.

What in the name of Totality could the Ronin possibly want at First Touch? No, he realized, it wasn't the Ronin, it was the Mind Brothers, or more correctly, Totality. What could Totality want?

Ignoring the possible danger that the Ronin around him presented, he dove even more deeply along the Mushin network, back to its diffused center, Totality. He searched and searched, looking for a reason for this strange migration to First Touch. What did Totality want there? What did it hope to accomplish?

When he found it, or rather a vague indication of it, it stunned him. It was beyond imagining. He opened his eyes and looked around him at the other Ronin who were becoming restless. "Come," he commanded them, his voice more powerful and determined than ever before. "Come, we go to First Touch. There is feeding."

Without another word, he turned and began to head toward the northeast. He would gather that group first, then swing west to add that one. Then they could come back east to get the others that were further south.

It would be difficult, might even entail challenges to the He-Who-Carries-Most of each group. But it must be done. The future of Kensho depended on it.

The rain had come with a sudden violence, lashing down at the earth and utterly drenching those who walked it. It also washed away any sign of their passing. Kristina held up her hand to call a halt. They had been jogging along at a pretty good pace for some time now and she knew it was extremely hard on Dunn. As she looked back, she could see how drawn and pained his expression was.

"We've gained enough on them," she declared. "I don't think they'll be on our trail any longer in any case."

"Do you think Erik can control them?" Dunn asked as he panted, trying to regain his breath. The pain in his leg was constant and throbbing. He was thankful to Kristina for slowing the pace.

The older woman laughed softly. "I'm betting my life he can hold them. I imagine he's very much in charge right now." She shook her head in wonder. "Never saw anyone change so much so fast. One minute he was dragging along as he has ever since he lost his Mushin. The next, he was the most incredible swordsman I've ever seen. And not only a swordsman. A leader. He became the *leader* of those Ronin."

"Do you suppose that's what He-Who-Carries-Most means? A kind of leader among the Ronin?"

Kristina shook her head. "I don't know. The one he killed didn't seem to be much of a leader, at least not in the way I think of a leader. Maybe he just controlled more Mushin and therefore had a stronger tie-in to Totality. Can't really say.

"But I *can* say that Erik became their leader once he killed that man. I sensed a distinct change in the relationship between them all. *Leader* is the only name for it. Don't you agree, Kim?"

The younger woman was looking back along their trail, a thoughtful expression on her face. She nodded in agreement, then turned and spoke quietly. "Yes. *Leader* is the word, but that wasn't what struck me the most. No, there was something even more amazing that took place back there."

Dunn looked at her, his whole face a question. "Something more surprising than being rescued from a band of Ronin by a Ronin?"

Kim nodded again and looked at each of them for a moment before continuing. "Yes. Even more unexpected.

"Didn't either of you notice that Erik said *I*?"

◎ Chapter 23 ◎

The Way-Farer nodded to Judah. "I understand your group's research has been successfully concluded?"

The young Plainsman smiled proudly in response. "Yes, Master. We have perfected the method of sending without a secured end point. We are now able to Snatch material to any point on the planet, provided, of course that the sender can visualize the location to which he is sending."

He slowly let his eyes drift over the members of the Council. There was a distinct look of barely suppressed excitement and triumph on his face. "But we have done more." Judah turned his glance to Josh. "We have done what you thought could not be done."

"Ah," he smiled slightly, "wrong again, eh? You mean, I assume, that you've found a way to transport living creatures?"

"Yes. The problem, you see, was that you had not thought the question through thoroughly enough. You tried sending lizards and when they arrived dead, you just assumed the procedure was hopeless. The real problem, though, was not the living creature, but rather the kind of living creature. Lizards, you see, are not sentient. Humans are."

"True," Josh murmured. "For the most part, true."

Judah ignored him and continued addressing the rest of the Council. "We decided that one of us had to volunteer to try to transport himself or herself to a destination we could picture but which was not anchored. I chose to be the one.

"After careful preparations, I gathered my Mind Brothers, concentrated their force, and tried to visualize a location on the Plain near where I grew up. When I had it firmly in mind, I threw myself there." He graced them all with a beaming smile of triumph. "Obviously it worked.

"You see, it isn't possible to Snatch a living creature anywhere unless they can visualize the location in their own mind. In fact, you can't *send* a living creature under any circumstance. They must send themselves. Which is why the technique didn't work with a lizard. The creatures aren't sentient and can neither picture the place they want to go, nor understand the use of Mushin to send themselves."

Judah turned once more to the Way-Farer. "Master, we have the weapon we need to defeat the Earth Fleet." He bowed and sat down.

For several moments, all the members of the Council sat quietly, looking down at the ground in front of them. Finally, Mother Cathe cleared her throat softly. The Way-Farer nodded in her direction.

"Ummmm . . . ah . . . Father Kadir, may I comment? Hummmm, yes. Well, Judah, I am sure we are all very impressed with what you have accomplished. I myself would have said it was impossible. Allow me to be the first to congratulate you and offer the sincerest thanks from all of us on the Council.

"I fear, though, that you pin too much hope on your discovery when you claim it to be the weapon we need to destroy the Earth Fleet." She held up her hand to forestall his protest. "I know, I know. I can easily visualize how you intend to use it. Send a group of armed Kenshites aboard each ship. Have them attack and destroy the Earth Fleet from inside. Yes, brilliant.

"I wonder, though, if you have considered two very obvious things? First, the person sending himself must be able to visualize where he is going. Pardon my skepticism, but I doubt highly that anyone on Kensho, with the possible exception of Dunn, can picture places on one of the ships Earth is sending.

"Second, the enemy is armed much as we are, even

aboard their ships. Myali saw that, and took part in a fight with their weapons. So we would have to fight, surprise or not. Furthermore, we would be fighting on their ground. We know nothing of the layout of the ships they are sending. It seems unlikely they will be similar to the scout Dunn came in, even less likely they will resemble the ancient flagship that circles our planet.

"So, while it is very tempting to believe that what you have found is a wonderful weapon, I for one do not see it as much more than a way of annoying and possibly damaging the Fleet."

The discussion went on for a good hour before Josh nodded to the Way-Farer and rose to speak. "Judah's work is to be praised, but like most of you, I don't see that it offers us any hope of beating the Earth Fleet. Somehow I feel it reeks too much of the tactics they would use themselves.   —

"I've always felt that the only way we could defeat the Earth was by inventing totally unexpected tactics, tactics so different from what they're used to that they wouldn't even understand them until it was too late.

"As most of you know, I spent a long time searching for something that would answer the need. As you also know, I failed, completely and utterly. So much so that I gave up and went Wandering.

"That was how I happened to stumble on the pattern of the mounds. I've brought that information before you but until now none of us have been able to make any use of it.

"Until now. Recently Dunn returned from his Wandering. Pretty much the worse for wear," he tilted his head in the Earthman's direction and gave a little smile, "but very excited. He also brought Kim and Kristina with him.

"The story he told and the information he brought was incredible." He chuckled. "Dunn and Kristina had to explain it to me several times before I could even begin to comprehend what it meant. Then I saw how it fit in with my own information, with the mysterious pattern of the mounds.

"Kristina has done a great deal of work with smooth-stones, has discovered that they generate some sort of *field,* for want of a better description. Smoothstones are found only where the mounds are. The pattern of the smoothstone field and the pattern of the mounds are complementary.

"Very exciting, but still rather esoteric. It was Dunn who brought it all together for us, and in so doing, may just have discovered the way to fight the Earth Fleet. I'll let him explain his idea. It's strange, shocking, possibly insane. I guarantee that the Earth Fleet won't be expecting it!"

Dunn shifted his weight off his lame leg and settled into a more comfortable position. This was going to take a while.

Two moons had set and two more were just rising when the discussion had finally ground down to an accepting silence. "Then there's no other way?" Mother Cathe pleaded.

Sadly and wearily, Dunn shook his head. "I wish there were. Josh and Kristina and I have gone round and round for a good week now and there doesn't seem to be any way out."

"But," an elderly man complained weakly, "to carry out this plan we'd have to drop everything else and turn all our resources to it. If it didn't work—"

"If it didn't work, we'd all be dead," Josh finished for him. "Yes, that's true. But what choice do we have?" The question fell into the dead silence of the night. What chance do we have? Josh asked himself once more. This insane plan based on a wild surmise? Dunn isn't even one of us. How can he be so sure?

Father Kadir looked at the Earthman. "Your plan requires great sacrifice from one individual. Have you any suggestions as to who that person should be?"

Dunn nodded slowly. "Yes, Father. I am the logical one." Kim started to protest, but Dunn raised his hand to stop her. "I know, you want to volunteer. For one who claims to be so afraid of losing her self, you're always the first to leap to any dangerous task. But, no, I'm the logical one. Odds are they have my profile in the computer and

would instantly be able to identify me. That would give
them a moment's pause, since they would assume their
bomb had been effective and blown me away. That
moment of indecision might be the key to the whole plan.
We need it. Just enough time to get them talking.

"Besides," he said slowly, sadly, "I doubt I'll be able to
be part of the rest of the plan. I have to have somewhere
to go afterward." Their silence expressed more than any
words could ever say.

"But can we do it?" Judah asked. "I mean it will take an
incredible concentration of Mind Brothers. At most, we
control perhaps a third of them. The rest are either free
floating or under the domination of the Ronin."

"That had worried all of us at first," Kristina answered.
"Then we heard from an old friend. In about a week's
time, a band of some two hundred Ronin will arrive at
First Touch." There was a gasp of indrawn breath from
everyone on the Council. "Don't worry," Kristina continued. "They're here for the same purpose we all are. Erik,
their He-Who-Carries-Most, is aware of the plan and
assures us of Totality's cooperation. Or rather that he and
his Ronin can manipulate Totality to meet our needs."

The Way-Farer chuckled. "What do you find amusing,
Father?" Josh asked. "Ah, nothing major, my Son. It just
occurred to me, though, that the history of mankind on
Kensho is ending much the way it began. The Mushin are
coming to First Touch and the two parts of the human race
that survived the massacre are joining once more. I'm sure
Nakamura would relish the paradox. I also imagine he
would appreciate the nature and elegance of the plan you
and Dunn are proposing."

"Yes, I suppose so," Josh replied. "Now if only it
works."

"You really have to do it that way, huh Dunn?"

The Earthman looked at Kim and nodded. "Makes the
most sense. You going back to work with Erik?"

"Uh huh. I . . . well, somehow that's where I feel more
comfortable. I mean, you know he's got a self now. A real
one. Oh, you should see him, Dunn. You'd be so proud of

him! He's their leader, just like Kristina said. He told me
to say hello to you and wish you the best. And he said to
tell you you were right all along . . . it does make a
difference. What's that all about, Dunn?"

Dunn chuckled. "Oh, just a little discussion we had a
long time ago. At the time I lost. Now I guess I've won.
No, I guess we've both won. You love him, don't you?"

It was too dark to see her blush, but the moonslight
suddenly shone brighter in her eyes and he knew the
answer even before she spoke. "Yeh, I guess so." There
was a gentle silence between them then. Finally Kim
broke it with a soft, pleading question. "Will it work,
Dunn?"

He looked at her in the dark, trying to read the
expression on her face. She wants it to work so badly,
wants there to be a future for her and Erik to enjoy. What
can I tell her? I don't know if it will work? No, not that.
"Sure, Kim, sure. It'll work. It's bound to."

She sighed as she stood. "I'm glad. Glad for all of us.
The thought that we might only have another year to live
is just too . . . too, well, too awful. I don't want to die,
Dunn, and not just because I'm afraid to. I've conquered
that now. I don't want to live as a slave to Earth, either.
I'm glad there's a hope we'll be able to defeat them and
live free."

She leaned over and kissed him on the forehead.
"Good-bye. Thanks for the reassurance." She began to
walk off. "By the way, Dunn, you're a lousy liar. But
thanks anyway."

The last two moons had set before she arrived. He was
lying on his back staring up at the tiny points of light that
marked the flagship and the arks. She sat beside him and
neither one spoke for a long time.

"You found what you were looking for?" she said at
last.

"Yes," he replied, "and no. It can't be found the way a
thing can. It's not like that."

"No," she replied, "it's not."

"In one sense, it's really there. In another, it's always

just passing through. It changes, grows, is never the same, but always constant, always there, always the same. A paradox, an enigma, but real nonetheless."

"So now you're complete."

He laughed. "No, hardly. None of us are. Oh, we are, but we're also becoming. We're the passage of the past into the future. Both exist and are transformed in and through us. All of us are equal in that. The gaps in my past are one of the things that forms my future, so in a sense they aren't gaps at all. I'm content and that's enough."

"But you're going to do it anyway?"

He shrugged. "Everyone asks that same question. Of course I'm going to do it. Who else? It's poetic justice in a way, I suppose. The spy comes back a spy. I hardly think they'll be expecting me. I'm simply completing the cycle they started. Once I've returned to the beginning, perhaps I'll start again."

"Doing what?"

He sighed. "I don't quite know yet. I have an idea, though. Look, if this thing works the way I think it will, well, there's going to be a lot of questions that have to be answered. Answering those questions could change a lot of things that no one ever expected would be changed.

"I've learned a lot here on Kensho. Some of it isn't too useful for us ordinary humans. Some of it is. I've got to sort things through, but there's a message to be delivered, one a lot of people will be interested in hearing."

"The Hierarchy?"

"Hardly! No, they'll want to keep it quiet. But that'll be impossible this time. Too much has happened. And with this new thing . . . well, it's beyond hushing up anymore.

"Things are changing. I feel that somehow I'm an important part of that change." He sighed. "Probably just a silly, egotistical dream but—"

"Ummm. Maybe not."

"Whatever. It makes it easier to think there's some future in what I'm planning to do."

Silence settled between them once again. It was a mellow, friendly silence, filled with love and caring. Finally, she stood. "So, then. I'll be going. I'm glad you've found so much. If this works I guess we'll all owe you a lot.

Thank you, from all of us." She turned and moved slowly away, blending gradually with the night. In a few moments, she was invisible.

Only then did he speak. It was a single sentence, a yearning whisper thrown into the vastness of the night sky.

"I love you."

There was no reply. He didn't expect any.

❂ Chapter 24 ❂

Admiral Knecht looked around the wardroom. The Commanders and sub-Commanders of the seven ships in his Fleet were all there as were their counterparts serving the Power. At least they were there in one sense. In fact they were still on their respective ships. Physical movement between ships in Aspect-Sarfatti drive was impossible. What were present were three-dimensional holographic images. The only real flesh and blood people in the room were himself, the Commander of the flagship, the sub-Commander, Cardinal Unduri, and Unduri's second in command, Bishop Wilson. The identical scene was taking place in every wardroom on every ship in the Fleet.

Knecht cleared his throat to call the meeting to order. "Gentlemen," he began, "we will be dropping out of A-S drive at oh-eight-hundred-thirty hours Earth Normal. The purpose of this meeting is to inform you of the intended actions to be taken at that time and to entertain questions you may have regarding that action. Hard copies of the complete plan are being transmitted as we speak.

"Now, we will enter real space in Corona formation." He turned to the wall behind him which instantly lit up with a representation of the Kensho system. "Flagship will take Jewel position, the rest spread out as shown. One and Two will instantly blast the ships that hang in geosync orbit here." He pointed to the representation, and the area he spoke of enlarged. "I want total destruction. I want it instantly. So far as we know, this flagship represents their only space-based means of defense. The two probes we

188

sent off have both returned and show nothing that would disprove this theory.

"It is assumed," he continued with a slight, dry smile, "that this action will notify the Kenshites of our arrival. Since we are unable to determine what, if any, defenses they have managed to establish since the last mission, all ships will instantly engage in evasive maneuvers. These maneuvers will continue until I give the word to desist.

"Naturally, if we meet armed resistance, Plan Roach goes into effect and each of you will perform your assigned mission. If resistance is stronger than Level Delta, Plan Armageddon instantly takes effect. Destruction shall be complete.

"Our expectation, I will remind you, is that the Kenshites will wish to negotiate. That puts Plan Overlord into effect. Three and Four will blast moons one and two. That should be a sufficiently impressive display of our power. The flagship and Five will strike designated population concentrations as per the probes. Note that these are quite small by all our standards, but the demonstration should be effective in any case. Six and Seven are to stand ready to launch Landers with their Marine contingents. The Marines will secure the necessary Touchdowns and the rest of the Fleet will proceed to off-load reinforcements.

"I estimate the entire procedure should take . . . ummmm . . . say five hours and thirty-five minutes or so. During that time any and all resistance from any source must be instantly and totally smashed. No prisoners, no hostages. Nothing. I want body counts and nothing else."

One Commander raised a hand. "Women and children?"

Knecht nodded his head emphatically. "Everything. Even hostile animals. The demonstration must be utter and total.

"Once the Touchdowns have been totally secured and perimeters have been set up, entertain contact with the first natives who approach. Kill them if you have even the slightest suspicion. If they genuinely wish to talk, and I feel sure they will by that time, have them transported to Touchdown A. The Cardinal and I with our respective staffs will have made our HQ there.

"Are there any questions? No? Good. Then the Power be with you all. Cardinal, will you give us your blessing?"

Unduri rose and stretched out his arms, his hands meeting over his head to form the circular symbol of the Power. "In the name of Reality, in the name of the Circle, in the name of the Power, in the name of Humanity. So be it and so it shall be."

One by one the Commanders and sub-Commanders signed off and disappeared from the wardroom until only the five true occupants were left. Unduri turned to the Admiral and spoke softly. "Swift and harsh. Very good, Admiral. Just as Kuvaz would wish it. This is the proper way to deal with dangerous heretics."

Knecht looked the Cardinal in the eye for several long silent seconds. Then he nodded brusquely. "Yes. It is the right way to deal with any dangerous enemy."

Dunn lay on his back, the thick grass of the hill cushioning him for the long night of waiting. In the nearby dark he could feel the presence of the others. They were all gazing skyward.

"Do you really think they'll do it that way?" Josh asked softly.

"That's what I'd do if I were them," Dunn replied absently. "Start off with a big bang to put a fear into the natives. Then talk. Of course, they might just come in shooting. In which case we'll have to move very swiftly or it'll all fall apart. You're ready with everything?"

"Ready," Kim responded. Erik murmured his assent. Dunn could hear the slight movement of cloth as Kristina nodded.

"Good, well then all we need to . . ."

Above them in the night sky the tiny dots that marked the locations of the flagship and partially dismantled arks suddenly flared into bright life. "Aaaahhhhh," they all breathed out, struck by the beauty and finality of it. "It begins," Myali added into the silence that followed.

"And ends," the Way-Farer said. "Dunn, my Son, we must part ways now."

Dunn nodded in the night. "Yeh. Let's get it going, huh? No time to waste." He was glad it was dark.

* * *

Admiral Knecht strode back and forth on the bridge, looking at the screens that displayed the view from his own ship and from all the others. They all showed the same thing. Nothing. And that bothered him.

"No sign of any resistance?"

"None, sir," came the crisp reply.

"Damn," Knecht swore under his breath. "Cease evasive maneuvers," he commanded out loud.

"Evasive maneuvers ceased."

The Admiral turned to face Cardinal Unduri, a frown creasing his forehead. "I don't like it."

The Cardinal raised his eyebrows in mild surprise. "In the name of Kuvaz, what is there not to like? The operation went off quite smoothly, Admiral. The ships were blasted, the maneuvers were executed like clockwork—"

Knecht cut him off with a chopping motion of his hand. "I know all that. Our side is doing fine." He turned and pointed at one of the screens which showed Kensho hanging serenely in space. "It's their side I'm worried about."

"But they've done nothing. They—"

"That's just the point. Damnit, look at all those sensors! From every indication, Cardinal, we are staring down at a primitive planet! This is supposed to be a Class Three, not a Class One! And what's more, they've had eight years since Yamada and Thwait were here. They should have been working like hell to resist us. But there isn't any indication of—"

"Perhaps I can help," said a voice from near one of the consoles.

Knecht spun to stare at the person who stood there. He was dressed in a travel-stained robe of coarse brown fabric. A sword was thrust through his belt. The hood of the robe was thrown back so the man's curly, reddish-blond hair was visible. Bluish-green eyes were set in a strong, solid, almost square face. The straight nose pointed to a mouth set in a firm, determined line.

Instantly, five laser wands were pointing at him. He slowly held up his hands and a sarcastic smile bowed his stubborn mouth. "Overkill, Admiral, overkill. I'm not here to fight, only to talk. You can have the sword if you wish. I don't carry any other weapons. And besides," he nodded toward his left arm, "I only have one hand."

"Who are you?" the Admiral managed to growl.

"Ask the Cardinal. I'm sure he's scanned me by now."

Knecht turned to the Cardinal, who was staring fixedly at the brown-robed figure. "Jameson, Dunn. Acolyte Third. Drive Engineer. Wiped. Restructured. Destroyed by implant on completion of mission. At least that's what the files say."

"But if he was destroyed . . ." the Admiral began.

"I said," the Cardinal interrupted, "that's what the files say. Obviously, the files are incorrect. Minus a hand and some of his leg, this is basically the same man."

Dunn bowed slightly. "More or less accurate, Cardinal."

Knecht turned and snarled at him. "How the hell did you get here, Dunn? There's no way into this ship. It's locked up tighter than a drum. We're on Red One alert. There's no way—"

"Damnit, man, quit blustering," Unduri cut in. "Of course there's a way. He's here, isn't he?" He leaned forward and glared at Dunn. "I don't care how, I want to know why."

A broad smile curved Dunn's lips. He was clearly enjoying the discomfiture of the two men and wanted them to know it. "We assumed," he began, "that the little display with the flagship and the arks was an invitation to come and talk. Were we wrong?"

" 'We'," the Admiral barked. "Who is 'we'?"

"Why, the Kenshites, who else? They wanted me to come as soon as you called to arrange the terms of your surrender."

There was a moment of stunned silence on the bridge. Then Knecht shattered it with a harsh snort of laughter. "Ha! Our surrender? Ha!"

Dunn nodded gravely. "Oh, yes. We assumed you would want to avoid the useless death of all your men. We are prepared to offer quite reasonable terms."

"You . . . you are what?!!"

"Admiral, Cardinal, what we did to the scout ship was a simple thing. We are prepared to do much worse things to this Fleet. If you surrender immediately, unconditionally, we will be merciful. Otherwise . . ." He shrugged.

Knecht and Unduri looked at each other in amazement. Then the Admiral looked back at the sensors. Finally, he turned and stared once more at the calm figure of Dunn. When he finally spoke his voice was soft and under control. "I don't think you or those who sent you quite realize the situation. You see, we have a Fleet of seven battleships stationed around your planet. All I have to do, Dunn, is give the word, and Kensho will become a smoldering cinder in approximately fifteen minutes. All life, Dunn, *all*, will cease within the first thirty seconds of that time. This is not an idle threat. I will be happy to demonstrate on one of your planet's moons if anyone doubts our power."

"And yet, Admiral," Dunn replied gently, his eyes locked on those of Knecht, "I was able to enter this flagship, this bridge, without anyone seeing or stopping me. Doesn't that give you something to reflect over? Think of what that might mean, Admiral."

It took Knecht less than a second to react. "Secure all corridors," he shouted. "Stand by to repel boarders!"

"All corridors secured," came the answer seconds later. Then a slight pause and a second reply. "No boarders discovered. All repelling crew standing by Red One."

The Admiral turned a baleful eye on Dunn. "What are you trying to do? You're bluffing, aren't you? You're here all alone. Your people don't have the wherewithal to send any more after you. You've discovered some means of transporting we don't know about, but that's all. It's just a bluff."

"I'm here to discuss your surrender, Admiral. We will take no military action until necessary. At this precise moment, it appears that none is necessary. However . . ." Dunn let the word hang in the air between them.

Before Knecht could reply, Cardinal Unduri held up his hand to forestall him. "Dunn," he said coldly, "for an emissary of peace and goodwill you seem oddly bent on prodding the Admiral to take action. I wonder why?"

"The Admiral decided we were sending boarders, Cardinal. I said nothing of the kind."

"No. But you intimated as much. I wonder, Knecht, if we shouldn't question this one on my machines."

The Admiral's distaste showed on his face. "No. We don't have time for that. Our orders are to subdue this planet quickly or to destroy it. To question this man would take time. That is precisely where Yamada and Thwait failed. I will not give these Kenshites any time to carry out whatever plans they might have."

"But Admiral," Unduri tried to sound reasonable, "there is data here we might need to make a decision. This man knows a great deal. In a few short hours we could probe him thoroughly and find out everything he . . ."

Knecht drew himself up sternly. "Cardinal, in my opinion we have no time to spare. This man's appearance on the bridge of this ship indicates that the Kenshites have means at their disposal which are clearly not in keeping with their status as a Class Three planet. The fate of the last mission reinforces that conclusion. I see no choice but to commence Armageddon immediately."

"Admiral, I protest—"

"Cardinal, I don't give a damn what you protest! This is my ship and my Fleet! My orders are to destroy this planet and I am damn well going to do it now!"

He turned to the control boards. "Commence Armageddon at once!" his voice rang out. "Blow that damned planet out of space!"

All eyes turned to the screens that filled the wall. Points of light suddenly burst out on the face of the planet, marking it with strange, fiery blemishes. The glowing points spread and multiplied until the whole orb was lit with a lurid blaze. A world died writhing in flames.

Victory marking every line of his body, Knecht turned to confront Dunn. "There, damn you! That's my response to your demand for my surrender! Your planet is dead! Your planet . . ." The look on Dunn's face stopped him cold, freezing the words he was about to speak in his throat.

Tears poured from Dunn's eyes. But deep within them was an unmistakable gleam of triumph.

✪ Chapter 25 ✪

Dunn leaned back on the cot and stared at the ceiling of his tiny cell. He didn't know how much longer he had to live, but he didn't want to interrupt the conversation he was holding in his mind. He'd held it so many times that by now it almost seemed as if Myali, Kim, Erik, Kristina and the others were actually there with him. I wonder where they really are? he thought.

The conversation was essentially a replay of one that had taken place on Kensho just a short time before the Fleet had arrived. It had started in the morning and lasted well into the night. He could almost see the stars as they had shone in the sky while they sat in the dark, winding up the discussion. He closed his eyes and it all came flooding back into his mind.

"So the pattern of the smoothstones in Kristina's cave is similar to the pattern of the mounds?" Kim asked.

Josh nodded. "Yes, the minute Kristina saw my drawing she recognized it, didn't you?" The older woman nodded. Josh continued, "The smoothstones and the mounds seemed to be part of the same system. Yet their functions appeared to be different."

Kristina took over the tale. "The smoothstones are part of an energy pattern. They both generate and are the field they generate. That field is interdimensional. The smoothstones are the manifestation of it we can see here in our space. The field itself extends much farther, perhaps to seven-space."

195

"I still don't understand the function of the field," Kim responded.

Josh took over again. "You have to go back to the pattern of the mounds. Of course, all this is conjecture, but it seems to work, so however inadequate, it'll have to do. Anyway, the mounds are a two-dimensional representation of higher-dimensional space. We think it's some sort of decoy to attract creatures of a higher dimension. Perhaps it's also a habitat resembling as nearly as possible the environment such creatures might be used to."

Erik spoke next. "That's how the species that used Kensho as a laboratory brought the Mushin here. The smoothstones are how they kept them here. You remember how my Mind Brothers were trapped in the pattern Kristina had in her cave? Well, the total pattern, following that of the mounds, acted as the walls of the habitat to keep the Mind Brothers here once they showed up. It worked. They came and were trapped."

"But," Dunn continued for him, "something went wrong. I guess the scientists just weren't prepared for what showed up. Even caged Mushin are dangerous. The creatures that built the trap ended up as food for those they trapped. Perhaps the shells of the Grandfathers are their remains. We'll never know.

"In any case, the Mushin couldn't escape to go back to their own dimension. No, that's not quite right. They are in their own dimension. What the trap did was to keep them fixed in this particular location within a cross section of the dimensions they inhabit. They weren't able to roam the multidimensional cosmos in search of food any longer. So when we humans came, they were very, very hungry for energy. You know the rest."

Kim nodded. "I think I see where you're leading, but go ahead. It's fascinating."

"Well," Josh took up the story, "both the Ronin and the rest of us became more and more accustomed to the Mind Brothers. Some of us began to carry the smoothstones. That disrupted the pattern, freeing the Mushin just enough to make things like Snatching possible. The field still held them here at this spot in this dimension, however. They couldn't move very far."

"Enter the threat from Earth," Dunn said. "A Fleet is coming to subjugate or blow up the planet. We have no way of fighting back. We lack the sophistication of Earth's weaponry. We're helpless. Whether we fight or yield, we lose. We find ourselves faced with the same kinds of impossible choices that Nakamura found himself faced with after humanity had almost been wiped out at First Touch. He couldn't stand and fight. He couldn't flee. He had to find a third way. We had to find one, too.

"It hit me shortly after Erik and you lost your Mind Brothers in Kristina's cave. I realized the smoothstone pattern had to have something to do with it. When I said I wanted to go to First Touch and tell the Way-Farer about it, you said we couldn't go because we had no Mushin, and it all came together."

"I'm sorry to sound dense, but I still don't get the connection," Kim said.

"Don't feel bad," Josh chuckled. "Dunn had to explain it to me several times. We travel by means of the Mushin. We're able to hold them to our minds, keep them with us, use them. We've adapted to them. In a word, we've become symbiotes.

"But the Mind Brothers are held here on Kensho by the pattern of the mounds and the field of the smoothstones. We can travel here and, because of the slight disruption of the field caused by some of us picking up and carrying smoothstones, we can travel in close proximity to the planet. That's why we were able to Snatch Myali back from the scout ship.

"Now, what would happen if the Mushin were no longer inhibited by the field? Presumably, they would be free to roam the multidimensional universe as they had before they became trapped here on Kensho. And we, as their symbiotes, would be free to travel with them! If the Mushin could escape from the trap of Kensho, so could we! That was Dunn's realization. The information I had gathered on the pattern of the mounds reaffirmed his theory and made it that much more likely."

"So," Kristina said, "we began to collect as many smoothstones as possible. We brought them all here to First Touch and began to reconstruct the pattern of the trap as fully as we could. At the same time, with the help of Erik and the Ronin, we gathered as many Mushin as we had under control and put them in the new pattern. That concentrated their power immensely. We learned many new things and developed new techniques of manipulation."

"But the key problem was still how to escape Kensho," Dunn continued. "Even when we disrupted the pattern of the smoothstones, the field continued to exist and to restrict the Mushin. Furthermore, the Mushin were still held by the pattern of the mounds. God only knows how long they'd been here, but in that time, like many captured animals, they'd grown used to their cage. The field of the smoothstones still existed, and the Mind Brothers actually seemed to prefer their habitat. We didn't know which was the stronger reason, but in either case, they refused to move and give us the means to leave Kensho.

"I'd suspected this might happen. So then we put our second plan into motion. It was drastic and more than a little frightening. If it failed, all was lost."

The Way-Farer nodded. "Yes. Many of the possible futures I had seen with Mother Illa had a similar ending. There was a good likelihood that the planet would be destroyed. There was no way to know if we would escape."

"The destruction of Kensho!" Josh said, his voice tinged with wonder. "Dunn understood what it meant! The destruction of Kensho was the destruction of the cage the Mushin were trapped in. Destroying the planet would set them free! And with them, us!"

"But how do you destroy a planet?" Dunn asked rhetorically. "Ta dah! Enter the Earth Fleet! Power enough to destroy ten Kenshos. And a noted tendency to do so. I've told you all about Quarnon several times.

"The trick was to get them to blast the planet rather than invade and subjugate it. The best thing would be to get some direct hits on the mounds and on the smooth-stones pattern to thoroughly disrupt them both. Judah figured out a way to arrange that by tracking the missiles and then Snatching them to the right locations. Oh, it's very complex. It takes an incredible concentration of

Mushin, which of course we have, thanks to the smooth-stone pattern here at First Touch. And some pretty incredible timing. Not to mention luck."

"One other thing," Kristina said, looking at Dunn. "It takes one person to go to the flagship and confront the Admiral. One person to make sure everything goes right. One person who cannot, therefore, escape with the rest of us."

Dunn nodded. "Yes. Me. I couldn't escape with you anyway. Oh, I can hold a few Mind Brothers for a short time. But I'm not adapted the way you all are. I'm not a symbiote." He glanced around the circle of solemn faces. "I'm the one who has to go."

The door to the room opened and Admiral Knecht entered. Dunn sat up and met his glance. Knecht took the only chair in the tiny cell.

For several moments, he sat silently, looking curiously at Dunn. Eventually, when he was ready, he spoke. "You know I've denied the Cardinal permission to put you under those damned machines of his?"

Dunn nodded. "I thought as much. I don't understand why, but thanks."

Knecht's eyes took on a more intense look. "I'll tell you why, Dunn. You're too damn valuable to let him destroy, that's why. You know things, things the Committee might be able to use."

"Like what?" Dunn asked, a slight smile playing around his lips.

The Admiral frowned. "Like why in the hell the Hierarchy is so damn frightened of Kensho. Like what was going on on that planet. Like what happened to that first mission. Like what happened to you.

"But most of all, what happened to all those people on that planet. Yamada's mission indicated there were more than twenty million people on Kensho, Dunn. Our own preliminary probes corroborated that."

"Ah," Dunn smiled broadly. "You've realized it was empty when you destroyed it."

"I've realized several of our first missiles didn't follow the trajectories they were set to follow. I've realized that suddenly several sensors changed their readings. I've realized the whole planet became empty in one instant while we were blasting it out of existence. I've realized the entire thing was some kind of setup, that you *wanted* us to blast that planet! I want to know why.

"Where are they, Dunn? Where the hell are all those people?"

Dunn's smile became smaller and gentler now. He shrugged softly. "Where are the Kenshites? Here, there, everywhere, nowhere. They have the run of the universe now, Admiral. They're freer than any human beings have ever been. They have unrestricted use of all of space and time."

A look of awe and wonder was beginning to grow in the Admiral's eyes. "I don't understand."

"No," Dunn replied. "I don't expect you do. What's more, I don't think I can really explain it to you. You'll just have to accept the fact that they're gone. They may come back this way some time. Then again, they may not. The universe is a pretty big place, and we're a pretty small part of it.

"But they left something behind them, Admiral. Something very important.

"They left us a Way."

❧ Epilogue ❧

The dawn sky arched blood red, colored by the light of an ancient, dying sun. It had already reached out and swallowed its three inner planets. On a hill above the tumbled ruins of a dead city, five robed and hooded figures stood in silence.

"Useless," one of them said softly. "This wasn't the home of the Experimenters. It's been dead for eons. Soon it will be swallowed by its sun. Useless. We should go on."

"On?" another answered. "We have gone on and on. The novelty is beginning to wear thin. So far we've found seven habitable planets. Our people are secure, scattered among the seven. Earth can never find them. And some day we will be mightier than anything the Power can muster to destroy us."

"There is no need to fight," a third said. "We can go where we wish. We have the freedom of the universe. Let Earth have its corner. The vastness can hold us all."

The second figure pushed back its hood. Myali's eyes met Josh's. "Have you forgotten Dunn?" she asked gently.

Josh bowed his head slightly. "No. I wonder if he still lives? Do you think they . . .?"

Erik shrugged. "Possibly. They can hardly have been pleased by what happened. They are bound to have blamed him."

Kristina shook her head. "No. I'm sure he's survived. They'd find him too valuable to kill. He's the only one in the whole universe who knows anything about us. They may have put him on their machines, though."

Myali smiled. "He knows how to resist. They wouldn't succeed. I agree with you, Kristina. Dunn is on Earth and alive. And with him the Way lives once more on the planet where it was truly born. He carries with him the seed which could very well do more to destroy the Power than anything we could do."

The five fell silent as the vast red sun rose over the horizon. It filled half the sky as it rose. Finally, having seen their fill of the dead world, they turned to go.

Erik paused and looked at the other four, a slight smile lightly resting on his lips. "Where next?"

There was no answer. All of them had the same idea.

Kim laughed. "I've always wanted to see the Home World."

With a slight pop, they disappeared.